Photo: Kaye Moseley

Merrilee Moss is a playwright and novelist who also lectures part-time in writing. Her plays, which have toured to theatres and community venues all over Australia, include *If Looks Could Kill*, *Empty Suitcases* and *Over the Hill*. Moss is the author of a number of books for young adults, including *Thriller & Me* and the eight-book adventure series *Hot Pursuit* — written in collaboration with Jenny Pausacker.

Other works by Merrilee Moss

Young Adult:
Thriller & Me (1994)
Hot Pursuit, Kristi (1993)
Hot Pursuit, Semra (1993)
Forget Me Not (1992)
Hot Pursuit, Franca (1991)
Hot Pursuit, Louise (1991)
Behind the Scenes (1990)
Best Friends (1989)
Hungry for Love (1989)
Stroke of Luck (1988)

Edited books:
Taking a Punt: First Stop Bonegilla (1997)

Plays:
SEZ WHO?! (1994)
Empty Suitcases (1993)
About Face (1991)
Over the Hill (1989)
If Looks Could Kill (1988)

FEDORA WALKS

MERRILEE MOSS

SPINIFEX

Spinifex Press Pty Ltd
504 Queensberry Street
North Melbourne, Vic. 3051
Australia
women@spinifexpress.com.au
http://www.spinifexpress.com.au

First published 2001 by Spinifex Press

Fedora Walks first appeared as a serial in *Lesbiana* magazine.

Cover design by
Edited by Barbara Burton
Typeset in Sabon by Palmer Higgs Pty Ltd
Printed and bound in Australia by Australian Print Group

National Library of Australia
Cataloguing-in-publication data:
Moss, Merrilee.
    Fedora walks
    ISBN 1 876756 04 7.

1. Crime fiction. 2. Ghosts in literature. I. Title.

A823.3

For Heather

Grateful thanks to
Helen Edwards, Barbara Creed
and Jules Wilkinson.

FEDORA WALKS

... INTO MY LIFE

I was in one of those grumpy moods when burning your fingers on the caffe latte glass is no longer pleasurable. That day I hated everyone — even Jodifosta, my beautiful blue heeler puppy. Normally Jodifosta would be nestled by the door of The Muff Café, waiting patiently. Normally just the thought of my loyal and faithful hound would send me spinning into a warm and fuzzy glow of happiness — but this was not any normal day. Oh no. This was the day my girlfriend's oh-so-tolerant mother had come to visit. The day I'd left poor old Jodifosta gazing sadly through the prison gates.

There are times when a girl just has to be on her own.

My Girlfriend's Mother (MGM) is worse than Jack Thompson's father-knows-best character in that movie *The Sum of Us*. Give me a break. Give me a good bit of old-fashioned prejudice. At least the bigots give you *space*. MGM's acceptance is like the slow squeeze of the python. I'm still gasping from shock. I knew we should have called the locksmith. I may never be the same. You see, MGM's not really tolerant. She's just plain old jealous of any other girl who plays with her baby.

This morning she decided to serve us breakfast in bed. There I was — riding high on a tidal wave of passion — when the door flew open. I still don't know whether the doona provided any visual protection for my flying breasts; I was too busy having a seizure. (Actually, I was too busy trying to merge the image of a grinning MGM balancing three steaming coffee cups and a jug of orange juice, with five lustful half-naked women, a gleaming Harley and me. But that's another story.)

MGM didn't spill a drop. Didn't avert her gaze. Left me a heaving wreck. My girlfriend Teresa leapt from the bed and cried defeatedly: *Mother!* I think MGM may have had the decency to gasp. I know I screamed.

It was the worst moment of my life.

... ON WATER

My fingertips were on fire and I was halfway through my second caffe latte when I saw *her* reflected in the mirror above the jukebox. I frowned. A soft grey hat tilted over grey-brown eyes. The woman was absolutely categorically and classically beautiful and she seemed to be staring at me. Me! A glimmer of memory — a sepia photograph — Katherine Hepburn in drag; then the image blurred. Was I seeing things?

'Julie!' Johnny threw his arms around me, obscuring my view. 'Julie Bernard! Oh, thank God for someone I know. I've been coming down from Midsumma for two whole days. It's been the absolute pits. I only took a teensy bit of ee... half a speed... but it's always like this. You want to die.' Johnny flipped his hair happily out of his eyes, sat down, grabbed my caffe latte, took a deep gulp, replaced the empty glass, then focused on my face. He glanced towards the doorway and back. 'Wo-oo... Think I'm still speeding... Where's Jodifosta?'

I cleared my throat. 'Did you see a woman...?'

Johnny was scrutinising the shadows under my eyes. 'You look almost as bad as I feel.'

'She was tall,' I continued, 'and sort of stylish.'

'No,' he said. 'I didn't.'

I felt my neck growing hot. 'But you must have passed her on the way in.'

Johnny looked puzzled, and then his hands slapped the table. 'You've got a new GF!' He announced in triumph. 'A tall, stylish one.'

'She was wearing a hat,' I added lamely.

Johnny's eyes gleamed. He nodded with approval. 'Hats are good.'

I sighed. What was the point? 'You drank my coffee.'

'I'll make it up to you.'

Suddenly, I laughed. Johnny always had that effect on me. 'MGM is in town.'

'Poor darling.' He leapt to his feet and aimed his body in the general direction of the bar. I observed lethargically as Johnny flirted with the waiter, wrapping his legs around the stool and begging for more coffee. My worries faded into the background. Perhaps I could just hang at The Muff for the next three days. With my real family. By then, MGM would be gone.

A silvery voice interrupted my thoughts. 'Excuse me,' it said with a distinctly French accent. 'Are you Ms Bernard?'

I looked up into a pair of beautiful grey-brown eyes and felt my stomach lurch. She was still wearing the hat. 'Yeah, sure,' I said, wishing I'd flossed my teeth, brushed my hair and washed my face. 'I'm Julie Bernard.' I held out my hand. 'At your service.'

'My name is Fedora,' the divine voice continued. 'I was wondering if you might do me a favour.'

Push-start your car? Move your fridge? Hang your washing? Save your kitten? Lick your feet? I shook my head, feeling the lust zones scatter. 'Yeah? And what might that favour be, honey?' I asked in my best Mae West accent. (I have always fancied myself a comic.)

The object of my desire settled neatly into the chair opposite and leaned forward.

'I seem to 'ave mislaid my… err… my 'at.'

I tried not to smile, but failed. What exactly had landed on my doorstep? A beautiful woman who couldn't find her hat — or even pronounce it. My eyes drifted over her glorious forehead to focus on the silky grey felt trilby hat hugging the crown of her adorable head. The corners of my mouth quivered with laughter and desire. 'Have you… err…?'

Fedora frowned. She appeared to have mislaid her sense of humour too. 'It was a turquoise 'at, with a deep green ribbon edge and scarlet plume.'

'Of course.' I felt suitably chastised. Another 'at. Another time.

'One wears it at an angle so that it tips gently over the left eye.'

I'm sure *one* does. 'Gorgeous.' I was beginning to suspect that I was dealing with an anal-obsessive neurotic with strong tendencies to narcissism and Dietrich delusions of grandeur, but it was too late. I was head over heels. Be still my heart. Mad women and I have merged before. I stared with fascination at to-die-for Fedora as she slowly pulled off her exotic tan-coloured gloves. Her fingers were long and fine; the nails short and filed. (Just how I like them. Moan.)

'So... err... Why me?' I asked calmly. Why the hat?

The script was straight from a movie. 'You came to me highly recommended,' Fedora said lightly. Then she reached into her pocket and pulled out a wad of notes. She stood up, pushing the money to my side of the table. 'Please do your best.'

'What do you mean, I came to you?'

Fedora gazed into my eyes and I melted again. She held up a hand. 'I will be in touch... soon.'

I couldn't help it. I had a squillion detective-type questions I needed to ask, but I glanced down at the loot for a moment. And when I looked up, she was gone. Gone. The woman of my dreams had walked in and out of my life, speaking in clichés and splashing cash. I was breathless with shock.

'Julie...? Is that you? What amazing luck! The Muff is absolutely chockers with dykes and poofs in recovery from Midsumma. Do you mind if we sit here?'

I nodded vaguely. Instinctively, I picked up the notes and jammed them into my jeans pocket. Five one-hundred-dollar bills. What is she really buying? What does she want? I rearranged my reality as The Clones sat down in Fedora's place.

My mates Jay and Maria are more than a couple of women who get off on wearing the same clothes. My mates Jay and Maria match exactly. Same glasses; same mouth; same nose-ring; same short brown haircut; same stories; same shirts; same massive mattressy mammary glands; same massive mattressy mammary love for each other; same laugh; same life. Of course, I love them to bits — but I just don't get the lesbian merge-thing.

I waited for The Clones to ask me about the gorgeous new babe I was seeing, but they'd been outdoors doing

5

something physical and they were more interested in food. *Have you eaten, Julie? I'm starving. Are you having a full breakfast, my darling? I don't know, my darling. We've only had toast and it's nearly lunchtime. Maybe a Muff Special. We could share it. Okay, my darling. I'll wave at Meg. We've got a friend working here. You know Meg don't you, Julie? I'll go over and order. No, my darling. You sit there and rest. Jay hurt her foot at softball practice. What, my darling? With sausages and avocado? Okay, precious. Hollandaise? Okay. What about you Julie? Julie! Honestly, the world is full of zombies today.*

My mind was racing.

I was wondering what it would be like to give up the concept of Self. I was wondering if The Clones had looked alike when they met or it had happened gradually. I was wondering how anyone could think of Hollandaise sauce at a time like this. I was also wondering where and how I was going to find that hat.

Jay was silent without her clone, and for a moment I was able to roam through the corridors of my enraptured mind in peace. We were staring vacantly into space when a piercing scream cut through the room, followed by the clapping of swing doors, running feet and breaking china. 'Call an ambulance,' someone yelled. 'A woman's OD'ed out here.'

I was dimly aware of Maria bursting from the swirling crowd around the bar. She fell into Jay's arms, half-kneeling on the floor. She was puffing — too shocked to speak.

'Julie,' Johnny whispered at my elbow. 'She's dead.' He sank into Maria's chair.

'Who's dead?' I hissed back. No. Please not...

Johnny's face was stiff and pale. 'That woman,' he sobbed. 'The one in the fancy hat.'

…Fedora.

… INTO A TRAP

I swear I didn't take another breath until my eyes focused on the filthy sole of a well-worn Blundstone. Despite our short acquaintance, I had already formed my impressions. I knew that Fedora would look ravishing in anything — but she just wasn't the type to wear chunky brown boots. A shaved head blocked my view… then jerked to the side. I heard a gasp. 'Blood.' Frightened words drifted on the breath of the crowd. 'Stabbed. Junky. Overdose. Ambulance. Oh, God. Who is she? Does anyone…?'

A tall thin woman in short shorts, studded dog-collar and a tee-shirt tight enough to expose her nipple ring suddenly took charge. 'Stand back everyone. Please go inside. Have a drink on the house. The cops'll be here in a minute. You might be walking on the evidence. She's dead. You can't do anything.' Suddenly, Meg noticed me and her eyes lit up. 'Let Julie through.'

I felt like a fraud as the crowd parted. Most of them knew me — and they all knew I'd never had a real case. Oh, I'd found the missing puppy. I located the perfect housemate for Emma. I discovered the closet marihuana smoker at Ping's house. I traced the keys to Johnny's car. I solved what is known rather hysterically as 'the case of the stolen sunglasses'. Once I even helped an adoptee (Emma's housemate) find her mum. But I generally live in a fantasy world peopled by V I Warshawski, Kinsey Mallone and Kay Scarpetta. I dream of jumping from moving cars and high buildings and drinking too much Johnny Walker on an empty stomach. Oh, how I long to find nothing but mouldering oranges in my fridge.

But I'm too well fed to be hard-boiled.

My limbs seemed stiff and awkward as I stepped through the crowd. I stood by the body listening to a moth battering in the wind. On that day, in that frozen moment in autumn, I knew I was all they had; a detective on a case.

I was guilt-ridden with relief. It wasn't Fedora.

The sky exploded and the rain came down, stroking the dead woman's face. I heard a dog's whimper — mine. I had never seen a dead body before — and this was a dead dyke body. Two buttons were pinned to the lapel of her brown wool jacket. One said, 'A Woman's Place is in the Mall' (even there — in that back alley contemplating death — the corners of my mouth gave an involuntary twitch); the other was more succinct, its message short and sweet: 'Butch Bottom'. This girl had had a sense of humour.

The body... How long ago had she been a person?... was half-twisted behind a green trolley bin, the head turned at an odd angle, staring blindly at the sky. I'd like to tell you that the woman looked peaceful, or even angry, but she didn't. She just looked sad. Her muddy caftan skirt was torn, revealing a small tattoo — a unicorn on her left thigh. Blood, which had formed pools in the cracks between the cobblestones, slowly diluted and disappeared.

I turned to the wondering crowd, clearing the rust from my throat. 'Does anyone know who she is?' Then I saw a familiar shape moving by the back gate. A trilby hat. I squinted into the rain, my heart at the starting blocks. Could that be...? Already I recognised the tilt of that determined chin. Fedora.

'Lily!' A woman with a mass of curling grey hair burst from the café and threw herself onto the body, screaming:

'Lily! Lily!' She lifted Lily's head and cradled it, keening into the rain. I know I should have stopped her — she was tampering with the evidence, but her grief was overwhelming. We wept silently until the police sirens took precedence and I snapped back to attention.

'What are you all doing out here?' a policeman bellowed. 'Don't you know it's raining?'

That was when I saw it. A flash of red... At first, I thought it was a scarf... but it was a long feather... A plume to be exact... It was attached to something soggy and green. I moved closer, folded into a squat and frowned. It was the turquoise-felt-hat-with-ribbon-edge-and-plume that Fedora had described. The hat she had paid me to find. Only this hat was not tipped elegantly over anyone's eye. This one was drenched; squashed flat against the stone. With two fingers, I peeled it from the muddy surface and turned it over. Inside the rim, a section of the label was still attached. I could just make out one word: *Pierre...*

Pierre. Who was Pierre?

I searched the dispersing crowd. I had two more questions. Where was Fedora? And what was a 'butch bottom' doing with a hat like this?

... THE DOG

That afternoon I did what I always do when my world collapses; I walked the dog. A terse note by the phone informed me that Teresa had taken MGM to the beach and I gulped the crisp air of freedom. I had promised to help out, but how could I honour such a promise? It's a jungle out there. I have crimes to solve; people to see; people to save. Sometimes a dyke detective just finds herself too busy for social niceties such as mother-minding.

For half an hour, Jodifosta and I paced the streets of Carlton, but the terrace houses seemed tiny and cramped; the streets overfilled with neatly clipped schnauzers and poodles on parade. My head was aching — bursting with images and sounds both real and imagined: blue flashing lights; a silky grey trilby hat; a never-ending scream; a blood soaked coat; the long shadow of a knife on an alley wall; an ambulance squeezing down a narrow lane. I couldn't breathe, let alone think. Who had done this terrible thing? Jodifosta was a ball of repressed energy; a coiled spring at my side. She could sense my mood and was playing it cool. She knew that it was time for the big spaces.

At Darebin Parklands we settled into a familiar rhythm. I charged purposely through the wet grass while Jodifosta tore in ever-widening circles after the rabbits of her mind. The sun streamed through the dark clouds, the air thick with the tentative optimism of autumn. On the bridge we passed a stout man with a white bull-terrier and I smiled inanely. His killer dog had nothing on my morning. A small waterfall attracted my attention and I focused on the sound of water running thick and brown over polished rocks. Good Feng Shui. I sat down with my notebook and began to list events chronologically.

9.05 MGM forces me from house. *9.55* Caffe latte at The Muff. *10.20* Divine Woman in trilby hat gazes at me from mirror. *10.21* Johnny — off his face. Drinks my latte. *10.23* Johnny flirts with waiter at bar. *10.24* Divine Woman introduces herself as Fedora. *10.26* Divine Woman asks me to find her turquoise hat. *10.28* Divine Woman passes me five one-hundred-dollar bills. *10.29* Divine Woman disappears. *10.20–10.30* Divine

Woman ploughs her way through my fragile and generally monogamous soul...

I refrained from noting the full extent of my feelings. After all, this was a detective's notebook — not a daily confessional. I chose not to write that I fell drastically and dramatically in lust with the aforesaid Divine Woman — with her silvery voice, her grey-brown eyes, her skin, her gloves, her well-filed fingernails — even her neurotic obsession with hats. I chose not to write that my ability to carry out my job was quite possibly under threat because of my burning and irrational desire to bite the Divine Woman's neck. I also chose not to write that I categorically refused to accept the glaring facts. But I knew in my heart of hearts that Fedora was quite possibly a murderer.

Suddenly icy cold water scattered over my face, jarring me out of my reverie. I screamed at the dog and tried to dry my hair with a hankie. Jodifosta grinned, then plunged happily down the muddy bank to dive into the creek again.

10.32 The Clones plan a hearty breakfast. *10.34* A scream — followed by much chaos in the vicinity of the kitchen. *Approx. 10.36* Johnny is sobbing, telling me that the woman in the hat is dead...

Panic resurfaced. For some reason, a wild surf was dumping wave after wave on my brain.

Approx. 10.45 Standing over Lily's body in the rain. *10.50* Holding turquoise-hat-with-deep-green-trim-and-scarlet-plume.

My headache seemed worse — the words were moving in and out of focus across the page and Jodifosta wasn't helping things with all that barking.

I looked up just as my dog began to howl. A figure was emerging from behind the waterfall — a figure in a grey trilby hat. I squeezed my eyelids shut and opened them again. Yes. She was still there. Jodifosta whimpered mournfully. It was Fedora...

Walking on water.

... OUT OF THE CLOSET

Fedora's fawn coloured leather boots hovered just above the creek's surface.

Jodifosta leaned her head against my knee and sank to the ground. She was depressed — and no wonder. There was Fedora, her image bubbling from the curtain of water like a laser image. My impulse was to scream, but instead I swallowed hard and willed my eyeballs to stay inside my head. One of us had to cope and Jodifosta was obviously falling apart. The wall of grey-brown rock opposite was just visible, shimmering through Fedora's body.

I should tell you at this point that I pride myself on being tougher than most. (That's why I'm a detective.) I can deal with: spiders; mice; rats; poo (except when I'm eating); vomit; snot (well — almost); blood; pus; real-life medical shows; maggots; snakes; scorpions; dead bodies; even the skin on hot milk. (I'm heaven on a stick to take camping.) But the supernatural... Well, let's put it this way — I still need a night light. And somehow I sense I'm no Dana Scully.

A voice started up inside my head. Loud logical reassuring phrases which challenged the erratic thump of my heart. Yes, Julie. This is really happening. No, it's not bloody Moomba. Look around you — no mass audience; no Fox FM simulcast. Broad daylight. Quite sunny in fact. Yes, that woman who calls herself Fedora is over there walking on water. Yes, she is transparent. No, you do not have x-ray vision. You are not Superdyke. You are Julie Bernard. You are quite safe. You are not asleep. No — you have not fainted. Neither are you dead. Look — you are still breathing. There is nothing to be afraid of. You are not in any pain. You are not crazy. You are not crazy! Are you listening, Julie? You are all alone with a very nervous dog and a… a… a…

Fedora shot toward us as if propelled by an invisible hand. I uttered a small scream. Then I lost focus, as her image fragmented, scattering like a horde of tiny insects before restructuring itself on the bank. Her vacant gaze drifted past my body and into the middle distance. Then suddenly… A flash of recognition and she winked. *Winked.* I was beginning to feel a little irritated.

'I'm terribly sorry to 'ave startled you,' Fedora said briskly. 'The transfer is generally conducted in private. I am not accustomed to being observed when…'

'How did you do that?' My mouth was hanging open. I was aware that I looked and sounded as if I was auditioning for a part in *Dumb and Dumber*, but at that point I was pleased to have the power of speech.

'I 'ad expected to materialise on that path — err — behind the trees.'

'Materialise?' I frowned. I have never been a science fiction buff, but this was beginning to sound like a *such* a cliché. I stood up and glared. 'Listen Ms… Fedora or whatever you call yourself,' I snapped. 'It's time I got some answers. A woman has been murdered.'

'That is exactly why I am 'ere,' Fedora said calmly. 'I am very sorry about what 'as 'appened, *mais*…'

'What's your role in all of this, anyway? You were at the scene of the crime. Don't try to deny it. I saw you skulking around behind the crowd. you…'

Fedora's eyes were aflame with indignant fury. 'I do not, 'ow you say — *skulk!* Do you know who I am?'

I have always loved a proud and passionate woman. I watched with fascination as Fedora's oh-so-elegant nostrils flared. A memory of the morning's desire resurfaced, but I chose to ignore it. (All right. I admit it. The possibility of her being related to ET had put me off a bit.) 'Who are you?' I demanded. 'It's time you answered a few questions.'

'I don't 'ave time to argue,' Fedora replied faintly. Was it my imagination — or was she quivering? Jodifosta gulped as a slow wave seemed to pass through Fedora's body — bloating first her cheeks, then her neck, chest and stomach. It looked as though she had swallowed a restless snake. What was wrong with the picture? I felt a vague urge to yell for the projectionist. I could barely make out her voice. 'Are you there?' she called. 'Julie! I'm losing you.' *You're losing me?* 'You must 'urry. There are lives at stake.'

Jodifosta and I stared wide-eyed at the talking paperbark. Fedora had finally flickered out. But a moment later her voice continued — distorting and crackling and echoing like an old radio in a tunnel. 'Look for my black... 'at,' she wailed forlornly. 'You must speak toooooo... @__"_-__#@$... Please 'urry.'

'Pardon?' I whispered to the damp grass. 'Speak to who?' I looked around self-consciously before raising my voice. '*What was that, Fedora? I can't hear you!*'

More static. Then a strange grumbling noise from the rockface and Fedora's voice spat a few more indiscernible sounds. 'Soup 'n undies... Sued bananas... Sue Fernandez'

Got it. 'You want me to speak to Sue Fernandez?'

Her last command was loud and clear. 'Find my black silk top 'at!'

Yes, ma'am. On the double. No worries. Piece of cake. Consider it done.

Ghost, genie, spirit or hoax — call me gullible; call me disturbed — but I was undeniably aroused by the concept of Fedora Walker in a black silk top hat.

… ALL OVER ME

I knocked on the frame of the fly-wire door, but there was no response.

According to Johnny, Toula Anderson lived in this rambling cream and green weatherboard in West Brunswick, but there was no sign of life. An image of Toula sobbing over Lily's body was now etched permanently on my brain. I peered hopefully through a small leadlight window. Damn. I had hoped she would be able to answer some questions.

I had obtained the basic facts from the police: Lily's throat had been cut (her death mercifully quick); Fedora's squashed turquoise hat had been filed as official evidence; they were investigating the possibility of homophobia as a motive. But the way I see it — squeezing info from cops is about as fruitful as seeking praise from my mother.

There's no point hanging around.

I picked my way through the long grass along the side of the house, cursing the strands of tangled jasmine. Around the corner an overgrown garden extended into the distance, ending with a row of white gums soaring at the sky. At the base of the back steps, an outdoor setting had been casually constructed out of two old tree stumps and a sun-bleached log. Farm girls. I smelt the warm bread.

Hippies. Thoughts of reiki, tai chi, lavender oil and crystals. I heard the soft murmuring of voices — even before I saw the massage table.

Toula Anderson was naked, stretched on her stomach in a patch of autumn sun while a tiny almost-bald girl with a single tuft of green hair worked furiously on her right shoulder. As I stared at Toula's porcelain white skin, I felt a nagging and uncharacteristic urge to study pan flute. 'Excuse me,' I said softly. Toula lifted her head, her eyes red-rimmed and swollen. The girl with the green hair stopped mid-stroke. 'I wondered if we could talk.'

Toula studied me a moment and then nodded. 'Okay.' She wrapped herself in a bright yellow sarong and tugged a red and black hand-knitted jumper over her head. Minutes later we were facing one another over the washed wood table and the girl with the green hair had flounced off to make tea. Toula lifted her mop of hair and arched her back with the grace of one who had danced under many full moons. But her skin was blotchy; her fingernails chewed to raw flesh.

'Tell me about Lily,' I asked simply.

Toula's lip quivered and her eyes filled with tears. 'I've been through this with the police.' She took a deep breath. 'What can I say? Lily was my ex. My friend. My confidante. She drove me crazy. She made me laugh. She was family.'

'Were you with Lily at The Muff on Sunday?'

She nodded. 'We met for breakfast. Then Lil gave me her script to read and took off for the loo. She's a... She *was* a performance artist. She took such a long time to come back, but I knew she was hung over and...' Toula put her head in her hands. 'If only...'

'You okay, Toula?' the masseuse called protectively from the kitchen window.

'You couldn't have done anything,' I reassured Toula.

Toula looked up — her face dark with fury. 'Don't give me that patronising bull-crap,' she hissed. 'Lil was out in that laneway alone! Alone!'

My gaze moved restlessly around the garden. I'm no grief counsellor, but I respected Toula's right to rage. Beyond the shed — I admired a lemon tree heavy with fruit. Above us — an ancient leafless grape vine, its stem thick as a thigh. Then my heart leapt. It was a thigh! Fedora was perched cross-legged on the broken lattice, her lips flapping frantically. 'Ask about the 'at. *The 'at!*' she mouthed silently.

I frowned. I had yet to develop the habit of communicating with levitating women. And, like most detectives, I preferred to work alone. How could Fedora be so insensitive? What if poor Toula looked up...

'Was Lily wearing a turquoise hat?' I asked Toula tentatively.

Toula sighed; her anger abating as quickly as it had come. 'Lil was a bit of an attention seeker. She had this thing about hats. She spent most of her time scouring the op. shops looking for new disasters.'

Fedora was gliding toward me. Drifting through the air, shouting silently. Her face contorted with effort. Surely Toula must see...

'That monstrosity was her latest find,' Toula concluded with a small smile.

Fedora's entrancing face was now millimetres from my own. Her tongue stretched toward my throat; my lips. I was mesmerised. Kiss or bite? Bite or kiss? Both alternatives seemed equally enticing. Then my back snapped upright as goosebumps tore from my oesophagus to my knees. For a fraction of a millisecond, Fedora's eyes gazed furiously into mine, then dissolved into blinding white.

'Are you okay?' Toula was asking.

White gum trees in the distance. A pale blue sky. Toula's look of concern. Fedora had disappeared — apparently by passing right through my body. Like Scarlett O'Hara, I decided to think about it tomorrow. Apart from anything else, the sexual connotations were mind boggling. And I had an investigation to conclude. Besides, I had finally read Fedora's lips. *'The black silk 'at!'* had been her silent scream.

'Did Lily have a black silk top hat?' I asked obediently, trying to appear calm.

'Yes,' Toula said, brightening up. 'And it's funny you should ask — because Sue Fernandez borrowed it this morning. She's doing a reading of Natalie Barney's works at The Muff on Saturday.'

... BACKWARDS OVER SAND

The Muff was buzzing. Everyone was there. Johnny was wrapped around a boy at the bar, sharing a cocktail. The lesbian filmmakers and their entourage were screaming about funding by the fireplace. Jay and Maria had brought the whole softball team and most of them were clustered around the remains of a chocolate mud cake. A couple of cloggers stood silently bow-legged by the door. Even Toula was there — sitting straight-backed with a solemn little group (including the girl with the green hair) next to the stage. I grabbed the last vacant stool by the window and tried not to think about my home life, which was going steadily downhill.

Teresa wanted us to have couple counselling but the idea made me queasy. I suggested hit-the-wall sex but she insisted that I was in denial and had serious problems with intimacy. Then she told me to get out and stay out. I said I was sorry and promised to help next time MGM was in town, but she said it was too late for 'sorry's. I said I had to go to a reading at The Muff, but even as I spoke I knew that was a bad move. I was putting my work before us and it was absolutely the last straw. Teresa accused me of running away and having no sense of commitment. She said there were 'serious issues' we needed to 'work through'. By that stage I was fed up and besides — I had a case to solve. So I did what I always do when the going gets tough — I slammed the front door.

The Muff had closed for three days after the murder. It opened again on Thursday, the coffee drinkers silent and twitchy with grief. However — life must go on, and by Saturday the audience at 'Kewl Girls' were desperate for distraction. There was a definite party mood, but voices were too loud, laughter too raucous. When the lights were lowered the anticipation was palpable.

A striking figure emerged in a cylinder of light. Stern stare — short dark hair — thick butch-beige leather gloves — dark brown jacket over crisp-cream-shirt-with-upturned-collar — gum-leaf grey jodhpurs buttoned over polished black boots. The *piece de resistance* none other than a black silk top hat with dusky satin ribbon tied casually to the left.

The Muff sighed a communal sigh of pleasure. Ah — we're back in stride.

'My name is Romaine Brooks,' the performer Sue Fernandez announced, her voice steady. 'Natalie Clifford Barney was my lover and life-long friend. I loved Natalie for more than half a century. We were Americans in Paris before the war — in those halcyon days of salons, private incomes and Amazon theatricals. I was a painter, Miss Barney a writer, but Natalie always prioritised living over writing. She always said, 'My life is my work, my writings but the result.'

'Romaine' paused for a cat-that-ate-the-cream smile. 'Natalie Barney was most attractive,' she continued in sultry tones. 'In fact, many of her sex found her fatally so...'

The audience was eating out of the performer's hands. Meg winked at me across a tray of dirty glasses, a stark millenium contrast in her lime green shorts, orange crocheted top and shaved head.

I stared at that black silk hat. This was a seriously weird case, but an idea was beginning to form in my mind. Lily had been murdered while wearing Fedora's turquoise-felt-hat-with-ribbon-edge-and-plume. Now Sue Fernandez was apparently wearing Fedora's black silk top hat. Was Sue in danger? Was it too silly to imagine a murderer driven by an obscure hatred of quality headgear. I toyed with the idea of leaping forward and wrenching the hat from the performer's head, but I sensed the audience might object. I glanced around the room. The crowd was entranced.

Once again I tuned in to the words of the notorious lesbian, Natalie Barney: I considered myself without shame: albinos aren't reproached for having pink eyes and whitish hair, why should they hold it against me for being a lesbian? It's a question of nature: my queerness isn't a vice, isn't 'deliberate', and harms no one. What do I care, after all, if they vilify or judge me according to their prejudices?

Images of women in hats and boots, carrying canes and walking with *strides* through the pre-war streets of Paris flooded my frustrated mind. Oh to be a literary lesbian way back then! (Even a literary lesbian's *friend*.) A time when women with money set up Salons — women with names like Gertrude, Natalie, Una, Alice, Radclyffe and Renee. Mm. Women who revered beauty and sensuality and loved, like Natalie, without jealousy or moral judgement. My head was starting to swim. I could feel a fantasy coming on. I rolled my shoulders in an effort to remain alert.

It occurred to me that a *Fedora* was also a hat. I made a mental note to look up 'hats' on the Net as soon as possible. Then I wondered why anyone would name a child after a hat. 'Hi. I'm Akubra. I'd like you to meet my daughter, Bowler...' Hmm... Maybe I could make it work. Beret Bernard, Super Sleuth & Dyke Detective. It would vastly improve my business card.

I was tasting the shape of my new name in my mouth when the spotlight swung rapidly around the room, then clattered to the ground, leaving us in darkness.

...BEHIND THE SCENES

There is nothing darker than those few seconds after blinding light. Instinctively, I leapt from my stool and began stumbling in the direction of the stage. Had I been right? Was someone using the darkness as a screen for murder? Was Sue Fernandez in danger simply because she was wearing Fedora's hat? My mind's eye conjured an image of figures struggling over a long sharp knife. My mind's ear (does one have a 'mind's ear'?) heard imaginary gasps, groans...

All around me was a seething fumbling tangled mass — lesbians in panic.

Suddenly I was flat on the floor between table legs, backpacks and a multitude of restless Blundstones. An ice cube tried to dig its way into my eye socket. Was that a knee or an elbow which dug savagely into my cheek? Cold fluid trickled down my back as I struggled to sit up. Was I the only one to witness the shimmering silver outline of a top hat floating high above the stage?

Meg's reassuring voice cut through the chaos. 'Lights please! Everyone keep calm.' Someone laughed — half hysterically. But dim light was returning, my eyes rapidly adjusting to the gloom. Somehow, my internal compass propelled me forward. People were frightened — scattering blindly, with no sense of purpose.

The tables cleared and a dark figure loomed before me. I dived for the ankles and knocked someone (screaming) from the stage. Then the house lights beamed and I noted that Sue Fernandez was struggling upright. A frizz of black hair spilled over her cheek. Fortunately, her fall had been cushioned by the crowd. She was hatless.

I hurtled through the stage door and past the lighting board, knocking over a hanging rack full of brightly coloured costumes. A red-sequinned number dragged my ever-wandering mind back to a happy moment with Teresa.

The New Year cabaret... We were watching Doris Day... Teresa was all frock and cleavage. I was leaning on the doorframe, my scarf thrown nonchalantly over my shoulder. A terrible nostalgic sadness threatened to drown me, but I was distracted by a couple of clothes hangers which launched an attack on my arm before rattling to the floor.

I turned a sharp corner and in the dim light the silhouette of a top hat drifted elusively in front of me. It didn't take much to deduce that a tall invisible person was wearing that hat. And there was only one person I knew who could become invisible at will.

Fedora had metamorphosed in the props room, and was draped calmly over a rather shabby chaise longue. The black silk top hat was beside her, balanced on a cushion.

I stopped and stared, breathing heavily. This woman ghost was driving me nuts. At every meeting, a system error seemed to occur in the software of my brain. *All coherent thought temporarily downloaded. Motor functions no longer functioning. Skin heating. Scalp tingling. Vision drifting. You have lost the power of speech.* All in the space of a few seconds. By the time I have drawn a second breath I am entirely absent but for a throbbing libido.

Fedora smiled. 'What an impressive job saving that actress! What a tackle! I do so admire an athlete.'

Naturally, I puffed with pride.

'You okay, Jules?' I turned to find The Clones peering curiously into my face. I nodded. Could they see Fedora, or did I appear to be talking to a hat? 'Everything's under control out there,' Maria soothed. 'Sue had just about finished her act anyway. It was excellent. We loved it, didn't we Jay?'

'Hey — great!' Jay enthused suddenly. 'You saved Sue's hat. She's looking for that.'

Maria stepped toward the chaise longue and reached for the hat, but it moved. Fedora had pulled it gently to one side. Maria froze.

'Leave the hat!' I commanded.

Jay and Maria stared wide-eyed. No doubt their reality

was somewhat different from mine. I can accept that. But I felt sure we all saw that hat move.

'Well, take it off that dusty old couch,' Jay warned. 'It's already fallen off the cushion and look at the floor — it's filthy.'

'Okay,' I agreed. 'But I think I'll just sit down for a minute. I feel a bit weird.'

Maria and Jay instantly grabbed an arm each and 'helped' me across the tiny room to the chaise longue.

Fedora patted her knee. I swallowed hard as I felt myself sit *through* her body. Hot fluid shot through my veins erupting in my stomach. Liquid fire — like brandy in winter. At the same time the base of my spine seemed to stretch, curling up and out like a scorpion's tail. I'd tried cybersex. I knew a person could be a figment of a combined imagination and still give pleasure, but this was ridiculous. Fedora sighed and moved a little to the right — languidly stretching beside me.

I waited till the sound of footsteps had faded before turning to Fedora.

'Okay, it's time for some answers. What's all this about hats? And who gave you that ridiculous name?'

... FROM THE PAST

Fedora frowned. 'Ridiculous?'

'Isn't a "fedora" a hat?'

'Yes,' Fedora replied coldly. 'It is an American version of the "trilby" actually — or the German "homburg". But this fedora 'at is named for me. Not me for it.'

'Oh.' I forced myself to stare at the back of my hand — clinging desperately to the familiar. I noted that the veins were becoming more prominent every day. 'How is that possible?'

Fedora tapped her fingers together. 'Too difficult for you to understand.'

I sighed. I had seen Fedora walk on water, then disappear and reassemble herself molecule by molecule on the riverbank. Five minutes ago, I had passed right through her body. How difficult could it be? 'Try me.'

'Well, Julie.' (I love the way Fedora pronounces my name. *Shoo-lee*. It sends me into orbit — makes me think of rain stroking leaves — somewhere south of Paris.) 'It's all connected with your great grandmother.'

That brought me back to earth. That was so *not* what I had expected to hear. 'My who...?'

'You were not selected at random, Julie,' Fedora continued, stroking the black silk top hat. 'This 'at — and all the others — belonged to your great grandmother, Julie Bernard.'

My jaw hit my knees. My tongue was itching to unravel across the floor like the mask in the movie *Mask*. 'They did?'

Fedora smiled. 'And now they belong to you.'

I held the rim of the top hat between thumb and forefinger, enjoying the cool elusive surface of silk. This beautiful object was mine? How did Fedora know that I had been named after my great grandmother? I was confused. It was an odd time to be offended, but my pride was hurt. I wanted to believe that Fedora had come to me because she needed a detective. Not because of my family connections. This was my first real case, after all. I dragged my mind back to the matters at hand.

'Who are you, then?' I asked abruptly. 'If you can float around in cosmospace — where's Greatgran?' I glanced over my shoulder half-expecting a female replica of my father to emerge from the wall. I was beginning to spook myself. I felt a brief urge to talk to Teresa — to lay my head on her shoulder and pour out all my troubles. But Teresa had thrown me out. I would have to go it alone.

'As I said — it's rather difficult to explain…'

I narrowed my eyes in challenge. 'As I said — try me.'

'"Try me",' Fedora mimicked affectionately. 'You Australian girls have such quaint expressions.' She leaned forward and ran a finger slowly down my cheek, smiling her charming smile. 'Don't mind if I do.' My skin bubbled, then opened like a sieve, blood pouring from a network of tiny holes. Very disconcerting.

Fedora was flirting openly. Another time, another place — and I might call her bluff, but this was a situation which called for control.

'I need an explanation.'

'We must find the other 'ats…'

'There are more 'ats?' (I was catching her 'abit.)

'Your great grandmother was very good about storing them. We left them in 'er charge when we…' Fedora bit her lip.

'When you what? *What*, Fedora…? Who's we? I can't work on this case if you insist on keeping me in the dark.'

'You look a lot like your great grandmother, you know.'

'Thank you.'

'Such an adorable little thing. Of course, we couldn't spend much time together… We were being touted about by that enthusiastic Williamson fellow… Interviews, parties… Publicity is such a bore, really.'

'When was this?' I interrupted cautiously. Please keep talking.

'When? Oh... About 1891 or '92, I think. The Australian tour. It was difficult, but Julie and I managed to meet up during the day. We walked and walked — exploring the city — for hours. Of course, that was before our accident.'

'Accident?' (I pronounced it the French way — *ack-si-dan.*)

'Silly really. Far too old to be jumping from parapets. Many years later... In *La Tosca*... A disaster.' Fedora's eyes met mine. 'You must have read about it?'

'Err... No.'

Fedora's lip quivered slightly, but she somehow turned a sob into a smile. 'Of course not. How could you? Anyway, we managed to stagger about fairly well with the use of a cane — even after they chopped it off.'

I gasped. 'Your leg?'

'Gangrene set in at the beginning of the war. But you don't want to hear about all of that. Besides...' She glanced down at her two beautiful legs. 'Time travel suits me very well.'

Pieces of a jigsaw spun from the whirlpool of my mind, slapping lightly against the movie screen inside my forehead — sticking like fridge magnets. A picture began to form. A woman who starred in *La Tosca* at the turn of the century. A performer who visited Australia — who knew... what was his name — Williamson... J C Williamson. Theatre producer extraordinaire. Who was she? The name was on the tip of my tongue. 'Fedora' just didn't feel right.

'Sarah!' I screamed. 'You're Sarah Bernhardt?'

Fedora nodded. ''owever, your great grandmother prefers to call me Fedora.'

... INTO MY DREAMS

I was going insane. What short circuit in my reality system made me believe that I had solved a case just because I had discovered that my client was a famous woman from recent history who had somehow floated through time and space in search of a few 'ats! How was it that I had come to believe that this aforesaid woman used to be best buddies with my great grandmother who just happens to be my namesake — Julie Bernard? *But that's not all — there's more.* This woman who had been coming on to me... (Oh, ghost who flirts!) claimed to be none other than Sarah Bernhardt.

It was all too much. My poor strained mind was in free-fall: first drifting in a formless frantic spiral, looping the loop, then accelerating in ever-diminishing circles, spinning through chaos towards the clear swill of the underworld. And down there in the dreamy depths, I added two and two together and determined quite conclusively that Sarah Bernhardt and my great grandmother had been lovers. My unconscious knew it to be the truth. (Wouldn't Jung be proud.)

This case was becoming so personalised. My greatgran. Far out. I was puffed-chest proud. Never thought of old Greatgran as a lesbian. But then, of course, I never knew her — and the only recorded facts are:

1. She was married with five kids
2. She made a great bread-and-butter pudding
3. One of her kids, Percy, was my granddad — my father's father.

If I was into family history (and I'm not), I'd have a really hard time because everyone tells a different story. My Nana (Percy's wife) called Greatgran Julie a feisty little fascist. (Maybe Greatgran Julie criticised her bread-and-butter pudding.) But my Mum assured me she was an Angel. (I guess that's why Mum gave me Greatgran Julie's name.) According to Mum, Nana and Greatgran clashed like Chris Evett-Lloyd and Martina Navratilova. (In the same ballgame, but never quite hitting it off.)

I resolved to research the subject in more detail.

I haven't seen much of Fedora over the last three weeks, but I'm not complaining. That girl takes it out of you. Anyway — I needed time to digest this latest blast from the past. Each new detail seems to slide my world further sideways. One day I'm going to tip over the edge.

But I haven't been idle.

I've been dealing with my home life. Call me a suck. Call me a sentimentalist. Call me a desperate and dateless. Call me a capitalist pig if you will. But I ordered a dozen individually wrapped red roses to be delivered to Teresa for Valentine's Day. Something had to be done. I've been pining terribly. I miss that gentle purr on the pillow at night. I keep having nightmares about Fedora floating on the ceiling. Jodifosta is complaining about our new conditions in Johnny's tiny terrace. His backyard is far too small for an active blue heeler pup. (Unless I take up marathon running.) Teresa hasn't exactly agreed to having me back yet, but she has agreed to have dinner with me this Friday. Yes! One small step for womankind...

Johnny and I go way back. He knows I like my toast buttered all the way to the edge. I know he likes skinny milk on his cereal. I don't mind if he hogs the shower. He doesn't mind dog hairs on the furniture. But most importantly, I don't mind his singing, which is very lucky because other flatmates have been driven to insanity. Half snatches of notes explode from Johnny's throat at full volume. He wears an invisible walkman and every now and then the music floods his brain, overflowing through his mouth. I can tell from the tone whether Johnny is happy or sad. It's a marriage made in heaven. If I was ever going to have babies (perish the thought) Johnny would have to be the daddy.

Johnny has state-of-the-art access to the Net and I've been in cyberheaven, staring at images of Sarah Bernhardt and imagining her with my greatgran. My client Fedora looks like Sarah Bernhardt, and yet she doesn't. It's like looking at identical twins. There's something butch about Fedora, but Sarah is all pretty poise and bracelets. Perhaps time travel causes a personality change. I have to say — I'm not sure of anything right now, but I'm working on it.

One thing I do know is: Sarah Bernhardt did visit Australia in 1892. And guess what! Her mother's name was Julie Bernard. Wow! Sarah's mum, my greatgran and me. That makes three.

Right now I'm off to talk to a milliner in the Block Arcade, Collins Street. Apparently Greatgran Julie used to 'frequent' the premises. Perhaps the milliner will recognise the black silk top hat. It's long shot, but worth a try.

... CENTRE STAGE

Life is too much. Living in cramped quarters with Johnny and Jodifosta, Teresa snubbing me in the street. (Sob.) Fedora spinning from the past, smiling seductively at each new curve. I am tempted to give up on this case, but I can't forget that a woman has been murdered. If chasing hats is going to help me find the culprit, then I will chase hats.

At least that was what I thought this morning. The tram into town was crowded and I was too self-conscious to wear the black silk top hat. (I leave such theatrics to people like Sue Fernandez. I'm a detective; we prefer shady locations on the edge of the action.) But standing in the crush of passengers, it became impossible to protect the hat any other way. It had survived intact for almost a century — and there was only one solution. I had to put it on my head. I felt a flush spreading through my cheeks to my neck. If Teresa could see me now.

I felt totally ridiculous, not to mention paranoid, and to make matters worse, something was driving into my lower back. Disgusting. I tried to wriggle away, but I was hemmed in by the swaying crowd. *Is that an umbrella or an erect penis?* I imagined myself saying loudly and clearly, but at that moment a sharp object tore through my shirt and the area around my right kidney burned. Realisation came slowly. I had been cut. Stabbed. Knifed in the middle of a crowded tram. The words 'flesh wound' flashed across that busy screen in my forehead. One could only hope. I turned, but there was no sign of the weapon and no one was moving furtively, trying to escape. I hate crowded trams. I held one hand against the injured area as I pushed toward the exit.

I felt a rush behind me as I jumped down the steps, and shivered. I had felt claustrophobic on the tram; I now felt over-exposed and vulnerable. I held my hand to my face, expecting the worst, and watched blood trickle down to my wrist. Maybe I'd knocked myself on the corner of a briefcase. Maybe I'd... But the tear in my shirt was too neat. I backed against a wall, my eyes darting about nervously. Someone was out to get me. I stuffed my handkerchief hard against the wound and tucked it into the top of my jeans. Fortunately, the cut wasn't too deep. I had been right. Flesh wound.

As I passed Parliament house, I heard footsteps behind me and turned suspiciously, but I saw only the solid stone wall and ascending steps. Then I looked with amazement at the huge painted sign over the theatre opposite. 'Fedora' it proclaimed: 'Fedora — Opening Tonight'. My mind buzzed like a beetle trying to right itself. I was incapable of coherent thought. I had to keep moving.

I hurried down the slope of Bourke Street hill, the echoing footsteps hurrying behind me. Fear pounded through my body, growing and throbbing with my heart. I began to zigzag quickly through the milling crowds. I was oblivious to the top hat balanced on my head. Terror took me across new borders — beyond fear of flamboyancy.

After the Russell Street intersection, I stopped. I was puffing wildly, my ears filled with the sound of my own breathing. I resolved to take up jogging (like V I and all the other detectives) and it occurred to me that Jodifosta would be pleased. I glanced behind me — up the hill. Office workers, Japanese tourists, a couple of kids in caftans, straights sucking face in the bus stop — everything looked normal. I felt sure that my pursuer had lost the race.

Then suddenly, I was pulled into an alley, punched in the face and dragged across the ground, my skull bouncing against solid concrete. I kicked out and was relieved to feel my foot collide with something soft. Flesh. My attacker was human. I grabbed a handful of hair and jerked myself sideways in an effort to see the face, but fat fingers were clawing at my throat. Seconds later I kicked again and watched with satisfaction as the knife spun across the lane and slid into the darkness of a drain.

The grip around my neck was tightening. Hot breath scattered across my face like an old fart. I was no longer fighting to survive; I was fighting for air. I was a rag doll, my limbs jerking at random.

Just before I blacked out, I noticed the hat floating to the ground and watched with detachment as my hand caught it in mid-air. Instinct. All that softball training at school — Jay and Maria would be proud.

It seemed only a few seconds later that I opened my eyes and listened anxiously to the snuffling whine of my own breath. I was alive. How? Why? I had been helpless, breathless...

I sat up slowly and took in my surroundings. A faint pink light mixed with the artificial glow from the street. Sunset. How long had I been unconscious? My hand brushed against a dark, soft object. The hat — half-flattened by my fall. I sat up and tried to gather my thoughts. The turquoise hat had been squashed under Lily... The first murder victim. She had been killed in an alley. I shuddered. The circumstances were almost exactly the same. If the knife hadn't fallen into that drain, would I be alive now?

My arm ached as I lifted my wrist into the light. 7.45... *Teresa! Dinner!* I was fifteen minutes late. All thoughts of safety left me as I tore out of the alley.

... INTO THE RISTORANTE

Teresa's face was thunderous, but I noted with satisfaction that she had dressed for the evening and a tiny part of my brain heaved a sigh of relief. Yay! She still likes me. She was wearing her best maroon silk shirt with her soft grey, tailor-made suit jacket with the fluffy collar. The one that goes with her maroon lipstick and her soft grey, tailor-made mini skirt. I love it when Terry wears her corporate gear.

I noticed Teresa's jaw clenching with fury as she looked me up and down. Here she was all dolled up for the big date and I had the audacity to turn up late — in filthy jeans, my face smudged and bruised, my backpack hanging miserably from my shoulder, my hand still clutching the bedraggled top hat.

What could I do? It was a choice between whining an apology — humbly informing her that being a detective sometimes means being held up by a bit of a scuffle — or kissing my beloved full on the lips, hoping to remind her of my irresistible charms and thus erase all memory of my lateness. Naturally I chose passion and for a moment, the surprise element worked in my favour. I felt a responding warmth as Terry's mouth opened slightly — her tongue pressed against mine. Oh, Terry. I want your body. Now. But then she was pushing me away — demanding an explanation, her eyes filled with pain and disgust.

I sat down, ordered an average-to-good cab-sav-merlot and began to tell Teresa everything. After all — what are girlfriends for, but to share the burden? If your path crosses a time traveller, if your head is spinning from too many unbelievable facts — including the exciting news that your great grandmother may have been as inverted as Radclyffe Hall — if you are desperately trying to solve a murder case — talk to your beloved. Who else is there?

The story poured from my lips in a raging torrent. It was such a relief to tell someone — anyone — I barely paused for breath. I told Teresa all about Fedora's strange and ghostly behaviour — all about Jodifosta's scare at the water's edge — all about the hats Sarah Bernhardt had left in the care of my great grandmother — the murderous threats that seemed to be associated with those hats — Fedora's time-travelling... Finally I came to my most recent adventures — being stabbed in the tram, then knocked unconscious in the alley. I couldn't eat; I was exhausted; I was babbling.

Teresa listened intently over her *fettucini fungi con spinaci*; she nodded over her *tira misu* and raised her eyebrows over her *latte*. I sipped most of the bottle of red wine while Teresa guzzled water in an effort to digest it all.

When she had finished eating, and I had finally run out of words, Teresa carefully wiped the edges of her mouth with her napkin, placed both hands flat on the table and said: 'You give me the shits, Julie Bernard. In case you haven't noticed, we're having severe relationship hassles and instead of dealing with them — you're escaping into la-la land. Well, you can play cops and robbers till the cows come home. You'll still be facing the same intimacy problems in the end.' She pushed her chair away from the table and stood up, a tear glistening under her left eye. 'I need a partner — a lover — a girlfriend, not some sort of crazy ghost buster! Not some would-be Nancy Drew! I think you need help, Julie Bernard. Seriously. Do you hear me?'

I was trying to think of an appropriate reply when the swing doors to the kitchen flew open and Fedora catapulted into the restaurant between two waiters. She glanced around, took a couple of long strides, and smiled at me over Teresa's shoulder. 'Go away,' I hissed. 'Now is not the time...'

Naturally, Teresa thought I was responding to her diatribe and her eyes boggled. 'When is the right time? You tell me, Julie! You tell me when you're not too busy rolling around in mud puddles, fighting your imaginary demons.'

'I didn't mean you, Terry. It's... Fedora. She's... Err... Have you met?' My voice trailed off miserably. I was confused. Terry looked absolutely radiant. A Collins Street goddess. Dressed for our favourite fantasy. I had a strong urge to throw her onto the table there and then. My mind's eye conjured an image of tablecloth, pasta, wine, coffee… overflowing to the floor. I would force Terry's thighs open… push that mini even higher…

At the same time, I was aware of Fedora's laconic and beautiful smile. Could she read my thoughts?

Teresa turned her head, following the line of my gaze. She frowned. The man at the table to my right was peering over his menu. The noisy family gathering by the door was almost silent. A dyke fight. Right here — out in the open. How exotic. How terribly twenty-first century.

Teresa took a step towards the door and shivered. And no wonder. She was standing inside Fedora. I stopped breathing while a few thousand horses broke loose in my chest. Fedora and Teresa — my two objects of desire — positioned in the one body. Eerie.

'I'm out of here,' Teresa's lips said from deep within Fedora's neck. 'I was prepared to give you a chance, Julie Bernard, but you haven't changed. My mother was right. You're totally selfish.' Teresa twisted her way out of Fedora's stomach, grabbed her bag from under the chair and slung it over her shoulder, hitting Fedora on the nose. 'Pay the bill — would you?'

My voice was a tremulous whisper as I called after her. 'Teresa…!'

… INTO THE WILD BLUE YONDER

Fedora slid into Teresa's seat, looking forlorn. 'I'm sorry, Julie. I do 'ope that wasn't my fault.'

I ground my teeth. Oh, spirit woman! What would you

know of the pain and trauma of temporal relationships? You can too easily escape to the comfortable haze of cosmospace, leaving us to stumble lead foot through life's amorous maze. (I sometimes have quite profound thoughts.)

Fedora's grey-brown eyes were moist with sympathy. 'I came as soon as I 'eard. But I have been busy — doing a little research of my own.' She reached over and stroked my cheek. 'Poor Julie. You 'ave been hurt.'

My heart thumped. Even in the midst of great distress, that accent drove me wild. Fedora's voice wafted like a Nina Simone song on a hot night — swirling around my thighs, breaking into a tango on my stomach — culminating in a barrage of riverdancing in the vicinity of my vulva. I wanted to dance on the table, but I felt I should maintain control. People were already staring. I now knew with absolute certainty (How bright am I?) that Fedora was invisible to all but me, and like Teresa, the other diners already had good reason to suspect I was a teensy bit unstable.

I rose, pulled out my wallet and ambled casually towards the door, trying to ignore Fedora. (Despite the fact that she strode beside me, her stylish suit and trilby a stark contrast to my torn and shabby clothing.) The waiter took my money and stuffed it into the cash register uncounted. I might as well have paid in used serviettes; his management was clearly desperate to see me go.

Hearing voices, seeing to-die-for dykes from the past — perhaps Teresa was right. Perhaps I was living in a fantasy world. After all, Teresa had not even sensed Fedora's presence — not even when their torsos had become one. I shook my head, feeling the bats rattle from the belfry. I was completely sane. Facts were facts. Fedora was a ghost.

I knew that. But she was a tangible ghost. Well — to me anyway. I could still feel the pulse of her fingertips — as if they lingered on my face. And Fedora had paid for my services in cold hard cash. (I'd already spent it on a few minor things — like survival.) You can't argue with that.

I waited until Fedora had climbed into my car before I opened my mouth again. By then, my indignation was the spring in a pinball machine; my words the tiny flying balls. 'Listen, Fedora… I've been stabbed, punched… What's going on? That guy in the alley was out to kill me. I'm still not sure why he let me live. My girlfriend thinks I'm a psycho. You appear and disappear whenever you damn well want…'

'You were wearing the black silk top 'at?'

I was furious. 'You mean you let me walk out there… a sitting target? You knew that if I wore that hat…' I was lost for words. 'I've had it. I'm over this case, Fedora. I mean it. It's too weird. You can take your fancy 'ats, and…'

'Please, Julie,' Fedora persisted. 'I did not think. We know that the murderer only strikes if the victim is wearing the 'at.' She straightened her collar. 'You must 'ave financial compensation for the danger. Poor Julie. The 'orrible pain you have endured.'

I gasped. 'You think this is about *money?*'

Fedora smiled her slow sensuous smile and handed me an envelope filled with one-hundred-dollar bills. 'I understand your confusion, Julie. Please. You must allow me to explain.'

I nodded dumbly, silently gasping at my sudden wealth. (Well — what am I supposed to do? I'm a professional. I can't just drop a case, can I? People depend on me. A woman has been murdered.) Suddenly, I felt claustrophobic in my tiny car. I wound the window down and took a deep breath of moist polluted air.

'I do not have very much control over my... err... travels,' Fedora continued. 'But I was looking for you. Some'ow, I managed to locate myself in the laneway at the rear of your little café.'

'You mean — when Lily was...?'

'Murdered. *Oui*. But my location drifted — I was only able to catch the tiny portrait. I wasn't there *exactement*. If you know what I mean. I saw the girl Lily wander into the laneway. She looked quite delightful in the turquoise hat with deep green ribbon edge and scarlet plume. A very attractive girl — although a rather odd assortment of clothing. Those boots!'

I *knew* Blundstones would be a turn off for Fedora! 'Go on. Yes? And then...?'

'Lily stretched up 'er arms. She paced back and forth. She seemed to be waiting for something — or someone. She was anxious, excited...'

'She was waiting for her friend Toula to finish reading her manuscript,' I cut in calmly. (A detective doesn't need to travel through time to collect her facts.) 'She'd been working all night to finish it.'

Fedora rested her head against the dashboard. She seemed to be running out of breath. Her voice was a torn whisper. 'Then a man — I think maybe I know this man — jumped out of an automobile — knocked 'er over — stabbed — and... *Poof!* It was so quick. I tried to maintain my position, but his awful vehicle was screaming toward me on the roadway. It was terrible.'

'And the turquoise hat was on Lily's head at the time of the attack?' I asked in my matter-of-fact detective voice designed to calm the witness.

'Oh yes. Most definitely.' Fedora began to sob quietly. 'If only I had been able to hold on, Julie. But without you as my focus, my anchor... I am lost. I was travelling blind — floating in an abyss of deep blue. When I am upset — it is even 'arder.'

I had the feeling I'd seen the movie. I stared at the dirty black silk top hat in my hands, a million questions queuing in my tired brain. 'What exactly do you mean... Without me as your focus?'

Fedora lifted her head, surprised. 'Oh Julie. Don't you understand? I am drawn to you like a magnet. Wherever you are... I would not be here at all if it were not for you. You have the name, you see... *Her* name.'

'My great grandmother's name?'

'Yes, of course. Your great grandmother, Julie Bernard. And our mother, *aussi*. Julie Bernard. Julie Bernard. Julie Bernard. You are the third Julie Bernard. *Trois* is a magic number, Julie. *Trois* is the Goddess trinity. *Trois* is the virgin, the mother, the crone. *Trois* is very 'elpful to me on the threshold. You understand?'

Mm. About as clear as mud. I'm not virgin, mother or crone... Johnny would probably understand. He's a trekky. But never mind. I get the gist. Only one thing... If you say my name one more time, I won't be responsible for my actions.

'You are a descendant of *une grande femme*, Julie,' Fedora concluded. 'Don't forget that.' She smiled. 'That is why I fell in love with her.'

Mm. All very interesting. I pulled out my notebook and pen. Always a good stabiliser. 'Okay, Fedora,' I said with resignation. 'I'm back on the job.' She leaned toward me and placed one grateful gloved hand over mine.

'So — what have we got?' I asked. 'A murderer who

goes after women wearing hats — specifically my great-gran's hats. Is that right?'

Fedora nodded solemnly. '*Oui*. That is right. And there are three more 'ats, Julie Bernard. You must find them! *Vitement!*'

... OVER THE RAINBOW

I didn't know where to begin, so I sulked at Johnny's for a couple of days, making notes and trying to reorder my thoughts. Johnny's the best. He ignores me — carries on regardless — to the point of stepping over me on the kitchen floor. I was in a serious slump, but it's quite impossible to become a major depressive — or even a couch potato, when you're responsible for a dependent and hyperactive blue heeler pup.

Some people eat when they're feeling flat, but not me. What's the point of eating when everything tastes like cardboard? I'd like to think this sort of deprivation makes me as hard-boiled as V I and Kinsey, but I've yet to beat my undetective-like aversion to whisky.

I was missing Teresa terribly. But what could I do? She had made her position quite clear: give up detective work, or say goodbye. A life-threatening dilemma. A detective needs a balanced relationship to come home to after a hard day on the trail. (Well, it would be nice.)

I guess I'm a relationship junkie. All my adult life has been spent attached to some girl or other. My love matches follow the inevitable pattern: break-up, pine (for a minimum of two weeks); fall desperately in love; settle down. It's called serial monogamy. Only once did I move on before the official break-up date — and although it was damned exciting at the time, the repercussions were gruesome.

There's nothing particularly unique about me. I'd like to be different, but attendance at my last decade party was eighty percent ex-lovers.

I know you're thinking my fascination with the glorious Fedora shows that I am unreliable, fickle and also not-to-be-trusted and treacherous, but I'm here to assure you that I hold my wandering libido in firm check. Despite my current dumped status, I am totally committed to Teresa. (Anyway — what could I possibly get up to with an intangible and elusive woman who not only floats through solid objects, but according to my unconscious, has 'done it' with my great grandmother.)

Back to the case...

I flipped through my detective's notebook and noted Toula's comment about Lily and hats. 'She spent most of her time scouring the op. shops...' Op. shops. Now there's an idea. Using my fingers to do the walking, I made a list of all the opportunity shops in town, added the costume shops, then — for Jodifosta's sake — began systematically to *cycle* from place to place.

Jodifosta and I travel well. I ride the road, while she conquers the path, stopping at every intersection. Jodifosta has a brain the size of the planet — and I'm *that* proud.

I'm telling you — there's a whole hat world out there waiting to be discovered. Before this case, my knowledge of headgear ranged from the red oval on the top of my parka in primary school to the madly exciting bicycle helmet the law now forces me to wear. Of course, I have had the odd urge for an Akubra when travelling in the Centre. Oh — and I know a bit about berets because Teresa wears them with such aplomb — with a blue and white striped tee-shirt. You know the look. It spells s-e-x-y and F-r-e-n-c-h and a-r-t-i-s-t all at the same time. (I guess it's in the genes. My greatgran and me — we both like French girls.)

Damn. I'm really pining now.

This investigation has expanded my vocabulary to include words like: mantilla, turban, fez, pill-box, tam-o'shanter, stetson, homburg, trilby, slouch, derby, bonnet, bowler, boater... and lots more. I have discovered gorgeous hats and ghastly hats and in-between hats. Hats I wouldn't be seen dead in and hats I'd love to see Teresa in. If I tried — I could probably develop quite an informed fetish.

I was two weeks further into the case and I still hadn't found any hats labelled 'Sarah Bernhardt' or 'Fedora', or 'Julie Bernard', or even the mysterious 'Pierre'. I was practically a milliner, my thigh muscles were beginning to bulge in my jeans and Jodifosta's beautiful blue-heeler smile had resurfaced, but I had nothing to report.

It was outside the 'Charismatic Costumery', located in off-off Chapel Street, that I finally had my big break. A rainbow flag was waving from the shop door and I was preparing to submerge myself in gay men's heaven when I caught a glimpse of Toula Anderson struggling out of a combi-van with a huge heavy-duty orange garbage bag. Her thick grey hair was twisted into a knot at the base of her neck and she was half-bent in ballet pose. I was impressed. (Please note: I said 'impressed', not 'turned on'. I am totally *committed* to Teresa.)

Jodifosta obviously recognised Toula's magnificence at the same time, because she rudely thrust her nose into her crotch — causing her to scream and lose her grip on the bag.

Coloured scarves and feathers and pieces of material spilled and bumped their way to the pavement, forming themselves into a pile of glorious, tattered, ribboned, multi-plumed, much-loved and much-worn hats. Of course! Why hadn't I thought of it before? These were Lily's hats. They had to be. Lily had owned two of Fedora's hats. It was logical that she would have the other three.

The girl-with-the-green-hair jumped from the car and gripped Toula's arm possessively. 'Get that bloody dog out of here!' The hair prickled on the back of my neck. (It's amazing how much you can dislike some people — on the basis of nothing.) She seemed rather small to be a bodyguard.

'Sorry,' I muttered.

Toula's face was solemn as she pondered the fallen debris. She tugged at a piece of rich green cloth until it came away from the mass. Gently, she pressed the ragged turquoise-felt-hat-with-ribbon-edge-and-plume against her cheek, then replaced it on the pile. I leapt off my bike. The police must have returned it to Lily's next-of-kin.

'Look, Clover,' Toula said, picking up a deep blue beret and dangling it from her fingers. 'Remember Girl Guides?'

I leaned my bicycle against the window and tried not to laugh. *Clover*. Would I think it was a cool name if it was attached to Toula. I turned to call Jodifosta to heel, but she was quivering against the wall. What now? Jodifosta was gazing up — in the direction of the rainbow flag. I didn't bother looking up. I knew who was there.

Good. Fedora could help me sort through this pile of hats.

... IN HIGH DUDGEON

Lily's collection had to be seen to be believed. 'I'll clean up this mess. Don't you worry,' I assured Toula. 'After all — it was Jodifosta's fault.'

The girl with the green hair snorted. 'Did you say, "Jodie Foster"?'

I raised my eyebrows. 'Mm. But it's spelt differently. *Clover.*'

It was out in the open. A mutual dislike of irrational but extreme proportions. If Fedora hadn't intervened at that point by floating down from her flagpole, Miss Clover might have been dead meat.

'Remember your manners, Julie,' Fedora murmured in my ear. 'The young lady is in mourning for 'er friend. We 'ave no time for argument. We must find the 'ats.'

My eyes were fixed on Clover, my forehead lowered like a bull. 'Nice name,' I said sweetly. 'Goes with your hair.'

Complimenting Clover was a brilliant tactic if I do say so myself. Better than a speeding bullet. Better than a ball of spit. She had Toula bundled into that combi-van in less time than it takes to say 'weed-killer' — leaving me in possession of the entire hat collection.

'Now what do I do?' I grumbled. 'How am I going to get all this home on my bike?' I was acutely aware of a cluster of middle-aged men with moustaches edging towards the *hats*.

Fedora seemed to have lost the plot. Her olive green trousers passed through the colourful jumble of felt and cloth without making any impression. She was a fragile Ophelia — her body bowed over each item as she touched it tenderly. She was muttering to herself: 'Styled to accommodate the cut of the collar... The signature of the more radical, forward-thinking... Fashionable... The essential accessory of the well-dressed woman... Such fine-tuned understatement... Ah, Julie... So refined...'

The men were advancing. They were muttering too. 'Vintage millinery!' 'Unbelievable!'

Trust my luck. Just when Fedora let a kangaroo loose (in the proverbial top paddock), I had to attract a bunch of happy little hat freaks. I had no time to waste. 'Do you recognise any of these?' I asked Fedora in desperation.

Of course, the boys assumed I was making conversation with them. 'Well... This gorgeous little dove-grey number is a velour derby,' a guy in short-shorts explained companionably.

Instantly, Fedora jerked upright. '*Vite! Vite!* That is your great grandmother's hat!' she screamed. 'That is Julie Bernard's hat!'

'That's my greatgran's hat,' I repeated, stunned. 'Thank you.'

'Exquisite,' another guy agreed. 'You don't get hats like that these days. Look at the subtlety. Grey silk scarf, grey netting, grey on grey. I hate the anti-hat sentiment of the 'sixties, don't you?'

'Sophisticated,' Fedora sighed with satisfaction. 'All held in place with a burnished metal buckle.'

'I'd say — about 1880. What'd you reckon, Tim?'

'Correct!' Fedora cried. 'Absolutely.'

I hate to talk in stereotypes, but trust gay men to know how to talk like catwalk comperes. 'Very clever,' I admitted, reaching for the hat. 'Actually, this derby was brought to Australia by Sarah Bernhardt.' (I know — it's pathetic. But my self-esteem has been slipping ever since I had to move out of home. I just couldn't resist a little name dropping.) 'She gave it to my greatgran in...'

'Enrico! Enrico!' Short Shorts shrieked — interrupting my moment of borrowed fame. 'A Borsalino beret!'

'Made of felt offcuts from the rim of men's hats,' Tim explained. Was there no end to their knowledge?

'To die for,' Enrico enthused. 'Was this also your great grandmother's?'

I didn't like to ask Fedora out loud in case Enrico and Tim and Short Shorts thought I was psycho, but Fedora answered as if she were a tangible part of the conversation. 'That hat is from a later time,' she said.

'They wore berets like that in the 'thirties,' Tim said as if in response. 'They were so poor — in the depression — they had to use anything they could find.'

Spare me the history lesson. 'Yeah — well, that's my girlfriend's beret,' I snapped. I don't know why I was feeling so threatened. Fragile ego, I guess. I squashed the beret into my bicycle pannier, blinking away an image of the beret curving seductively over Teresa's left eyebrow.

Choke. If I ever see her again.

After that, it was a free-for-all. Drivers stared from their cars. Pedestrians took wide berths to avoid us — as we (Tim, Short Shorts, Enrico, me and Fedora the friendly ghost) made ourselves busy — searching for buried treasure.

'Am I beautiful?' Enrico asked after a while. We turned to see him posed in an afternoon hat of black velvet. It had a small flat brim, trimmed with patterned silk ribbon, and bird-of-paradise feathers. There was also a brown plush tricorn with a flattened crown, set off with a 'V' of *aigrettes*. (You see — I too can speak like a milliner when I try.)

'World War One,' Tim said with authority. 'And, yes, you do look beautiful.'

'You can have that one if you like,' I said generously. 'I'm only interested in my greatgran's hats… the rest will end up in there.' I pointed at the 'Charismatic Costumery' door.

'What about this one?' Short Shorts asked hopefully. He was holding up a delicate green Florentine straw hat with a round crown and wide brim, completely covered with ostrich plumes, silk flowers and *faille moire* ribbons in shades of rose, green and golden yellow. It was slightly crushed, but basically in good condition. 'There's writing inside,' he said, squinting. It says… *Fedora*. Hey, Tim! Isn't that the name of the show we're seeing in town tonight?'

I lunged at the hat — almost tearing it in half in my enthusiasm.

Everyone yelled. Including Fedora. 'Careful! Careful!'

'Yep — that's the play,' Tim (the source of all knowledge) said. 'Hey — that play was originally written for Sarah Bernhardt…' He frowned — then beamed at me. 'These hats *really* did belong to…'

I nodded, feeling a wild stab of pride.

But Fedora was glaring at me. '*Fedora* has a season here?' she shouted. '*Fedora*, the play… is showing in Melbourne…?'

I nodded again.

'Why didn't you tell me? Come. We must go to the theatre at once!' Fedora was flashing on and off like a faulty neon light.

'But… Haven't we got one more hat to find?' I asked meekly.

... ME HOME

I pedalled slowly down the Punt Road hill towards the Yarra, Jodifosta racing along the footpath at my side — Fedora steadily swimming — in an odd sort of breaststroke — through the air above me.

If not for the seriousness of the crime (and the fact that I was being paid handsomely), I would seriously consider abandoning this job. As a detective, I am always grateful to have a team — but a ghost and a dog! I mean, much as I love them both — it is verging on the ridiculous. What ever happened to the ex-alcoholic side-kick with the rough manner and many contacts in the underworld?

We were heading for the city to find:

1. the theatre showing the play called, of all things, *Fedora*;
2. the one remaining hat: an elusive boater of wood straw — trimmed with a wide ribbon of patterned blue silk and a cluster of fruit and flowers, finished by a coloured veil which falls like a net over the face.

Intricate detail — yes — but when a case reveals that people are being killed while wearing particular hats, you can't be too particular.

I extracted this information from the mutterings which scattered like rain from above. Fedora was talking to herself — her tone urgent, brisk — one might even say *manic*, and for once I was grateful for her invisibility. Imagine the chaos if the drivers witnessed Fedora doing this fine impression of Mary Poppins on speed!

In contrast to Fedora's obvious agitation, I was chuffed with success — my bicycle panniers stuffed full of the hats we had found. Only one more hat and the case would be closed. The hat freaks had insisted I wrap each hat in tissue before laying them carefully in the panniers — but the Borsalino beret I had saved for Teresa. It was inside my shirt, next to my skin.

Moan. Teresa. Where are you? When will you beg me to return?

As if on cue, Jodifosta took a quick left, rounding the corner at the lights. I realised too late that her stout little blue-heeler legs were on automatic pilot and she was making a beeline for our old home with Teresa. 'Jodifosta!' I screamed, but a large truck drowned my voice. Damn. We would have to abandon Punt Road and take the back streets to the city. I pressed my lips together and made a pathetic attempt at a whistle, lifting my bike over the steep gutter. Fedora accepted the change of direction gracefully, sinking lower and lower until she was skating beside me — millimetres above the concrete. She looked fabulous. Such style and grace. I tell you what — Fedora has my vote for the Winter Olympics.

Jodifosta was out of sight. Why can't I whistle? What sort of lesbian am I? Let alone *butch?* Surely whistling is a pre-requisite.

My mind rolls with the rhythmic whirl of the wheels. As a detective I am the owner of the gaze — that's just the way things are — which in traditional/stereotypical/formulaic terms means I can be none other than butch. I would love to challenge convention and be one of the first femme detectives (queer or straight; male or female), but I seem to have a certain predisposition...

I am more comfortable adoring and admiring girls, than being adored or admired. I wear only black socks. I lean on door-frames with my hands in my pockets and my scarf thrown nonchalantly over my shoulder. I do not posture and flutter and shop — or whatever it is truly femme girls do. (I'll have to ask Teresa about that. If she ever speaks to me again.)

Of course, I treat all this butch-femme stuff with a post-modern deconstructivist and very queer sense of irony, but at the same time — and as I pedal furiously through the park — I must acknowledge the obvious:

— I carry a wallet (never a purse).
— I look like a drag queen in a frock.
— I can't (and won't) dance backwards (Teresa and I started our lessons with Dance Cats, but... sob...).
— I am obsessed with ironing (only a true femme can get away with that oh-so-sexy crumpled look).
— I drink beer from the bottle.
— I often call my friends 'mate' (and I have never worked for a union).
— I take up space when I sit (no crossed ankles).
— My fantasies take me into the realm of *me big strong shoulder look after...* rather than *me so little cry soft tears...* (Do I reveal too much?).

I do, however, have my limits. I draw the line at spitting long distances, for example. Although I do rather admire that sort of activity when carried out by a DT (duck-tail) butch.

But I digress.

Jodifosta lead us a merry chase. It was fortunate Fedora had no idea that we were going in completely the wrong direction. I caught a glimpse of Jodifosta's tail once or twice, so I knew my hunch was right, but she kept that little bit out of sight. I guess she was trying to tell me something. The poor little puppy wanted to go home.

When we arrived, Teresa was standing at the gate frowning and Jodifosta was sitting behind her on the doormat looking as if she had never left. I dug my hand into my shirt and pulled out the beret.

'Thought you might like this,' I said in a gruff butch monotone. 'It's a Borsalino.'

... THROUGH THE WINGS

Teresa's eyes scanned the surrounding air suspiciously. Could she see Fedora draped elegantly over the fence post? 'Are you alone — or did you bring your imaginary friend?' she growled.

'I found it at 'Charismatic Costumery',' I persisted. 'Why don't you try it on?'

Teresa was not so easily charmed. 'When did you learn the difference between a Borsalino and a bike helmet?'

I chose to ignore her (not entirely unwarranted) animosity, despite the temptation. (After all — it takes two to tango. I learnt that at Dance Cats.) 'So... err... What have you been up to?'

She glared at me, squeezing the beret in her hands. 'Mardi Gras. Sydney. Party. Party. Party. I have a *life*, you know.' I felt a twinge of jealousy. I had been so preoccupied. How could any self-respecting lesbian forget Mardi Gras? 'I was a dyke on a bike,' she said, twisting the knife.

'Oh.' I resisted the urge to ask for more detail. I know how much I can take and I was already in agony. Teresa didn't ride — which could mean only one thing. She had been one of those half-naked femmes riding pillion, waving at the crowds. *Sob.* I stole a glance at Fedora, but her head was turned away, her trilby hiding her eyes. Her shoulders seemed to be shaking slightly. Could she be *laughing*?

Teresa brushed some imaginary dust from the beret, then scratched at a white mark. 'What's this — bird poo?'

I smiled — the eager puppy. 'That means good luck, doesn't it?'

Teresa sighed. 'What are you doing here, Julie? What do you want? Why is *your* dog on *my* doorstep? Are you asking me to dogsit — or *what?*'

Oh dear. This wasn't looking good. Teresa was very angry and I didn't have a lot of time to hang about mending my relationship. I had a job to do — a client waiting impatiently on the fence. We had to get to the theatre.

Teresa was waiting for an answer, her face thunderous. Had she already forgotten me for some leather queen — a tattooed gym freak Sydney biker? I stared vacantly ahead — silenced by my confusion and a growing sense of grief.

It wouldn't do to mention the case — or Fedora. Teresa already thought I was losing it. She was completely over my work — completely over the whole idea of being on with a detective — even though in the old days it used to turn her into a bubbling panting mass of need and desire. (Why is it the things which turn us on initially, inevitably become the things which turn us so totally off?) I couldn't mention the last missing hat. I couldn't mention the fact that lives were in danger.

And that didn't leave much...

Teresa turned and began to walk into the house. 'You're a complete pain, Julie Bernard. Just take your dog and piss off. Get out of my life.'

I gulped. Surely — that was a little harsh. Was my relationship really over? My mind drifted immediately to a depressed bedsit slum. I stepped over the crazed and starving rats to get to my mouldy mattress. I was drunk. A half-smoked fag hung from the corner of my mouth. I was in Brooklyn — *Brooklyn...?*

'Do and say exactly what I tell you,' Fedora instructed, her face pressed firmly into mine. 'We will win your lady back again.' *Lady?* 'Trust me,' Fedora insisted.

I nodded inanely. Anything. I'll do anything. My mother always said I had the common sense of a chook.

Fedora launched herself from the fence in a sort of pirouette and suddenly she was on one knee — the gallant musketeer. '*Vite!*' Fedora commanded. 'Kneel, Julie! Kneel!'

I slid onto one knee obediently, feeling like the nerd of the century. '*I love you, ma chere,*' Fedora said and nudged me in the ribs. She was gazing at Teresa's retreating back.

'*I love you, ma chere!!*' I shouted. Teresa spun around, her eyes popping.

'*I miss you… ma fleur. I want only to be with you. You are my life. Ma coeur — err — my 'eart is broken — err… I am so un'appy without you. I love the deep mystery of your 'azel eyes, your lips are like… err … warm cherries, like pinot noir at a picnic in the sun, like …*'

I was caught in a bad Yoplait advertisement, but I ploughed on — my words mixing with Fedora's — her French accent softening my tongue — until I wasn't sure where her words finished and mine began. Teresa was staring. She was walking back down the steps — apparently entranced. It was *working*. I was beginning to enjoy myself.

'Do not reject me, *s'il vous plait*. Allow me back into your 'eart. I cannot live without your love. I will cook for you. I will wash your feet. Your 'ands are the 'ands of Mozart, your feet Margot Fonteyn, your legs are so long and strong and…'

'Oh ple-eese!' Teresa snapped. 'Get up. The McDonalds are watching. Bruce will hurl another rock…'

'I love your mother,' I concluded, rising to my feet.

Teresa roared with laughter. 'You're lying through your teeth — as usual. Ever thought of taking up acting? Where did you get that fabulous French accent? You drive me crazy. You're nothing but a macho man trapped in a lesbian body. What about daily communication? What about responsibilities? What about...?'

'I'll go to the therapist with you,' I interrupted. 'If you can put up with my obsession with work, I'll... I'll even stop brushing my eyebrows with your toothbrush.'

'*What?*'

'Just kidding. But I mean it, Terry. Let me try. I'll come shopping at the market with you, buy organic, wipe the benches... I'll even promise to help entertain MGM.' Behind Teresa, I could see Jodifosta gazing at us hopefully. Her life was being restored — her parents reuniting. 'Look at Jodifosta. She misses you. She loves you... too.'

Teresa studied me dubiously. 'Are you still seeing ghosts?'

I lied through my teeth. 'No. Of course not.'

'Come Julie. We must go,' Fedora whispered.

'Look. I've got to go into town kind of urgently,' I muttered. *Please understand*. 'Could you look after Jodifosta? Just for a couple of hours? Could I come back and talk. Alternately — could I come back and have wild passionate sex with you? I'll bring the Merlot.'

Julie! Fedora was shocked. But I was tired of being subtle. Fedora would just have to learn to appreciate our blunt millenium Australian ways.

After a meaningful pause, Teresa lifted both hands to her head and pulled the beret down over one eyebrow. My heart leapt. 'Okay,' she said simply. 'Eight-thirty. But if you're not here — *and* focused — I'm over it. I mean it.' Her jaw twitched. 'You're not the only fish in the sea.'

Ominous words.

'I love your beret!' I shouted as I cycled around the corner. 'And I love you, Fedora!' I shouted into the air.

... THE TIGHTROPE

An hour before the performance, the well-dressed theatre crowd was spilling onto the pavement. 'Meet you inside,' Fedora's disembodied voice instructed as I locked my bike to a road sign. 'I will see you in the wings.'

People drew back prune-faced as I pushed past, their mouths pursed like chooks' bums. Why label me 'homeless, hopeless — tragically unemployed'? Why dismiss me as a representative of the great unwashed unable to afford the eighty-dollar ticket? Why not bohemian, artiste, unemployed-but-soon-to-be-famous-actor? At the very least, detective-with-attitude.

My nostrils provided the answer. After my long (and sweaty) ride through Melbourne, it was quite clear that I was totally out of place. But I had more important questions on my mind. I had no time to mingle. I had to figure out how to get into the theatre and find Fedora. (She who walks through walls.)

A small door in the back said 'Staff Only'.

'Excuse me. Sorry. Sorry, can't you see I'm carrying a pannier full of hats. 'Scuse me. 'Scuse me. 'Scuse me.' My pannier wasn't the easiest of items to carry when rushing through a crowd of people poised for viewing and being viewed *avec* champagne glass, so of course a few of them were upset. (Glasses, that is.)

My traitorous eyes were drawn to a woman in a gloriously skimpy black evening gown. (Note the passive tense — i.e. I am not responsible.) Oh, the delicate contours. The body beautiful. Arm muscles bulging in delightful contradiction. Another champagne glass hit the deck as I came to a sudden halt.

My fickle passions were quite clearly aroused, but the vision-in-flesh was surrounded by men, and had that 'I-am-totally-straight look'. Other factors stopped me from making a complete fool of myself: a) I had an important case to solve; b) Fedora was waiting for me in the wings; c) I stunk to high heaven. Nevertheless, I had to resort to emergency measures, mentally revising the lesbian safety rules.

When confronted by a straight woman:
— Do not maintain your gaze.
— Do not engage in dialogue.
— Do not imagine that she understands your lifestyle.
— Do not allow that fantasy button to be pushed.
— Do not imagine that she will do anything but dabble.
— Do not imagine that she will do anything but play with your affections.
— Do not imagine that you have the slightest chance.
— Do not imagine that you will survive the experience unscathed.

Straight women. Who needs 'em? Sure, they need me and my debonair noble gallant ways — my caring nurturing versatile fingers — but only until the next man comes along — or until they become desperate for family approval, or they want his baby... Or whatever it is straight women want. (Freud never figured that one out either.)

Self-protection impelled me towards the door — away from the crowd and through a darkened office. A collection of plastic frogs toppled from the top of a computer monitor and hopped under the desk. Damn. I had to get my bearings. Moments later, I was in a rabbit warren of narrow corridors. How to find the wings? How to find the stage? Unlike my great grandmother, I never had a particular fascination for the theatre. But I was beginning to sense the excitement. I could feel urgency in the hushed voices murmuring behind closed doors. There was something exotic about the mix of sounds and smells. Someone somewhere sang a few bars of 'Fly Me to the Moon' and for some reason, it felt great to be on this side of the curtain.

The stage was in semi-darkness, but I could just make out Fedora balancing on a rope strung between two beams. She was doing a very good impression of a circus tightrope walker. She appeared, in fact, to be having quite a good time.

'Where is she?' a prima donna yelled through the darkness. 'Why can't I rely on anyone around here!'

A young woman pelted across the stage holding a bundle of frocks, and a hat. *A hat!* The last missing hat — unless I was very much mistaken. There it was — a boater of wood straw trimmed with a wide ribbon of patterned blue silk and a cluster of fruit and flowers. The coloured veil trailed behind.

Instinctively, I moved into her path. The woman was flustered, breathless. She looked at me curiously. 'Excuse me, I'm late,' she said just like the White Rabbit.

'Follow that 'at!' Fedora commanded from above.

... A FINE LINE

'Can I help?' I asked in a moment of inspiration.

I thought I detected a faint glimmer of hope in the girl's eyes. 'Who are you?'

'Oh... I'm just Julie. The work experience girl.' *Just?* I held out my hand, but withdrew it immediately. Not only were her arms full of clothes, she was carrying The Hat. 'I'm here to assist the Assistant Stage Manager.'

'Okay,' she said with a sudden smile. She believed me. 'You can take this hat to room nineteen. Tell Katherine I'm... I'm...'

'Flat out with a million little things and you'll pop in later?'

'Yeah — that'll do,' she said, passing me the precious boater. 'Thanks.'

That was easy... I turned The Last Hat slowly around in my hands, smiling to myself as the girl's heels tapped efficiently into the distance.

Fedora stood in the wings, clapping silently. 'Well done, Just Julie. Well done. What a performance! You were so 'umble.' She laughed and I bowed theatrically — waving the hat and bending low — like a musketeer. My first moment on stage and the accolades were already pouring in.

A girl could get used to this.

But I couldn't afford to relax. Time was ticking relentlessly on. 'Is the case solved now, Fedora — or what? I'm in a bit of a hurry. Got a hot date with Teresa, remember — at eight-thirty.'

'Of course. But first we must take the hats all together, and... *destroy them!*' Fedora has such a flair for the dramatic.

'Sure. No worries,' I said dubiously. Destruction is so extreme. 'We could stop on the bridge and...' I glanced down at the stylish boater. The hat looked so sweet, so innocent, so... antique. What had it ever done? 'I guess we could throw them over.' My voice trembled and tears sprang to my eyes. I saw the five hats, sodden and drowning, struggling to stay on the surface of the world's only upside-down river.

I had finally metamorphosed as a hat freak. Placards flashed across the curtain; words spun around the rim of the boater. 'Save Hats; Not Whales.' 'Eat Shoes; Not Hats.' 'Millinery is Mercy.' 'A Hat is a Hat is a Hat.' 'Hats of the world unite.' 'Women, hats and children first.' 'What do we want? Hats Forever. When do we want 'em? Now!'

'What do you think you're doing?' A mad-woman with makeup as thick as wedding cake icing lunged screaming onto the stage. 'Give me that hat — at once! Where's Kylie? Who are you?'

I stood my ground. 'I have to give it to Katherine. Are you Katherine?' I asked innocently.

Katherine narrowed her eyes. Wild flames of anger sprang from her orange hair, threatening to ignite the curtain. Apparently I'd given myself away. She must be *really* famous. 'Get out of this theatre at once!'

'Okay,' I said agreeably. 'See you!'

I jammed the newly beloved hat on my head, plunged off the stage, around a curtain and down a short run of stairs. Katherine's well-oiled voice screamed behind me: 'Stop that girl! My hat! She's taken my hat! How can I perform now? Oh, I can't go on!'

Fedora's nasal French tones joined hers in an elegant foghorn. (I know that sounds like a contradiction, but when Fedora yells, she sounds sort of like Piaf — but even louder and with less melody.) 'Take off the 'at, Julie! It is too dangerous. Take it off!'

I heard the urgency in her voice, but the hat stayed on my head because I was standing, mid-stride, knees bent in freeze frame — looking out and up... into a sea of faces.

Half the audience was already seated; the other half were making their way down the aisles. Everyone — even those half squashed between seats, balancing coats and programs — absolutely *everyone* was staring at the suspicious looking dyke detective who had rushed through the curtain wearing an ancient summer hat — clutching an overloaded bicycle pannier.

It was the definitive pregnant pause and (to coin a phrase) the audience was listening. Stupidly, I added to my guilty appearance by running very quickly up three stairs, pausing to pant slightly, then running very quickly down again. Very stupid. Very stage-struck. But no-one screamed: 'Throw out the infidel!' Instead, there was a sophisticated rustling and whispering and a fluttering of paper as people, embarrassed to be caught arriving late, settled themselves for the show.

They thought I was a performer doing the opening number. They thought *Fedora* had begun.

A cry came from a seat near the centre door. 'Hey, isn't that the girl we met at "Charismatic Costumery"? It is! I'm sure it is!'

... RIGHT PAST ME

'*Girlfriend!* Where did you get that boater? Love it! Simply — adore it.'

I waved idiotically at my new friends, the men-in-moustaches — and they started nudging people, their voices rising in volume.

'We know her! *Hello, darling.* Over here! Autographs, please! Why didn't you tell us you were an actor? See that talented lesbian down there on the steps. The one in the boater of wood straw trimmed with a wide ribbon of patterned blue silk. *We know her!* Why just this afternoon...'

I must say, they all looked very cute adorned for their big night out in bow ties made of rich red velvet — flowing black capes — lots of eye-shadow and, in one case, a particularly beautiful purple frock. They were half falling over the seats in their excitement — clutching each other as they reached for the stars. (In this case — little old me making my debut performance.) And as they cried out, they merged — all boundaries of self forgotten in their *joie de vivre*.

I felt a surge of rather queer pride. Those gay boys were so high on costume — on the sense of freedom engendered by a night of living the stereotype — they formed a living portrait. Its caption was contrived, deliberately subversive and clearly underlined by their very 'seventies moustaches. It spelt *Screaming Queens*.

That's another thing about the theatre — it has no closets. Love that!

I do wax lyrical at the strangest of times, don't I? But as we all know, quite differing thoughts can race through a brain at the same time — like, in many parallel universes. And in that one moment — when I appeared to be frozen with fear at the base of the stairs in full view of an expectant audience, my brain was very busy.

In one universe, I was devising an intricate, but still to be refined, escape plan.

In another, I was panicking about being late for my *oh-so-vital* date with Teresa. (I could *feel* the clock ticking towards eight-thirty, and I still had to buy the Merlot.)

In another, I was admiring my new friends — and in yet another, I was philosophising about gay and lesbian lifestyles.

Am I a genius, a Slider — or *what?*

But sometimes — you just have to quit making up weak excuses for inaction and bloody well *focus.* Especially when you are jarred out of your reverie by an official-looking person in a classic black three-piece suit descending the stairs rather rapidly, his eyes fixed on you in an *I'm-going-to-throw-you-out* manner.

Obviously not everyone thought I was a part of the show.

By this time, I clearly had one problem and one problem only: *Which way to run?* I was a rabbit frozen in the shooters' spotlight — my eyes fixed wide in terror and procrastination. If I ran towards the stage, Katherine — the prima donna — would rally her troops. My eyes darted from glowing exit light to glowing exit light, but I knew I was no Paul Hogan. I couldn't turn sheep dog and run over the mass of humankind.

Perhaps my millinery mates could provide a distraction. I was trying to articulate a request more specific than 'help', when the man in the suit suddenly turned his furious eyes to the stage. My big break. I lunged at the stairs, jumping two at a time — wishing I had never smoked dope. I was vaguely aware of spontaneous clapping and laughter, but I ploughed on. The suit looked puzzled as I shoved past. Then he laughed.

What was so funny? Me?

I tripped over a large zebra-bag protruding into the aisle and as I was struggling up, I glanced at the stage. Fedora was floating in front of the curtain — wearing a red-and-white-striped jacket, a straw boater and white shoes. She appeared to be tap-dancing in mid-air — using a cane with the skill of Ginger Rogers. I made it to my feet, but spun a full circle as the official seized first my upper arm, then my pannier.

I blinked... Of course — the crowd were watching a magician's trick. An invisible tap-dancer. Very clever, Fedora. Up there for thinking. Ten points. The crowd roared its appreciation as I yanked the pannier out of the grip of the official and stumbled up the stairs.

I pushed the swing doors open and dived between two attendants. Luckily, they too, were transfixed — roaring for more. Obviously the show as-it-was had been boring them stupid. It must be a nice change to see — what? The ghost who taps? Oh, Fedora — we will market you yet.

For a few precious seconds, I was alone in the foyer — free. Then there was a fluttering of many wings and a sweet acrid smell — like jasmine in full sun. Something black and soft — with the texture of an old flannelette blanket — wrapped itself around my face and neck and began to squeeze. I dropped the pannier and began to tear at my throat, but found — *nothing*. My nails (short, of course) tore at my skin, squeaking against one another, searching for the source...

Something was obstructing my breathing — but *what?* An odd hissing noise above reminded me of a cat we had once. Was it me, dying? All I knew was, I was running out of breath — running out of *life*.

The veil over my eyes cleared slightly and I watched an attendant take out his mobile phone and dial in slow motion. I screamed the number internally, *9...1... 1...*, but chastised myself immediately: you've watched too many American movies. I could only hope the attendant knew the emergency number in Australia.

I have to stop choking and get out of here.

Suddenly, there was a terrible hacking, clapping sound. The death rattle? *Oh, Teresa.* Then I thought I made out a word — a hollow, echoing song buried deep inside a melodic guttural churning — like a cow playing a didgeridoo inside my ear.

Give...

It was a word — followed by another, and another. Strung together, it became a repeating chorus — until I had made out a whole sentence. I didn't understand it, but I *felt* it — and it chilled me to the bone.

Give... me... back... my... love.

One more squeeze to my screaming oesophagus and I was released. Cool clear air-conditioned city air filled my injured throat. I could breathe. I could cough. I had waited — and *yes*, I could exhale.

Fedora ran past me, whipping the boater from my head. 'Hurry up, Julie. They are coming. *Vitement!*'

As I dived out the door, I saw the clock. Seven thirty-six. Fifty-four minutes to dispose of the hats and meet Teresa. Wild passionate sex — I will find you yet.

... WITH GREATGRAN

Approximately seven minutes later, I had my bike unlocked, the pannier attached, helmet on my head, and I was flying down Bourke Street — caught in the nether world of haste — somewhere between escape and joyous arrival. I was running *away* from that terrible velvety suffocating presence — rushing *toward* my girlfriend, my hot date and my old life. Meanwhile, I was lapping up the moment with each push on the pedal. After all — I was alive, and after a near-death experience — that can often be all that matters.

I presumed Fedora was somewhere in front of me, but I was too busy avoiding cars, trams, tram-tracks, pedestrians, Clydesdale horses and Clydesdale poo, to pay much attention. However, as I turned into Swanston Street, a large man in a black suit, a laptop over his shoulder and a briefcase bumping on his hip, began screaming and pointing upwards. He had noticed the boater of wood straw moving rapidly above the throng of people crossing Collins Street. I agreed that it might look a tad odd — a hat moving of its own volition — especially when taking into account the almost complete lack of wind. But I was privy to a fuller view, and noted Fedora anxiously strutting ahead as I crossed Little Collins. At that stage, she was moving just a little above the level of the pedestrians' shoulders, holding the hat high — like a flag in front of her face.

Fedora disappeared into the portals of Flinders Street station, and the large man laughed at himself and shook his head rather too roughly.

I lifted my bike over the gutter and joined the crowd on the zebra crossing. But Fedora was re-emerging. Damn. Where to now? Had she forgotten my heavy schedule? Her soft fawn leather boots were almost in contact with the floor as she strolled beside a young, tanned girl-of-many-piercings. When the girl stopped to bot a fag from a bunch of young travellers on the lower steps, Fedora appeared to be listening intently. Suddenly, she glanced up and waved the boater at me.

A blond American boy with red-rimmed hooded eyes spotted the hat, rolled his eyes full circle and sighed with pleasure. *Awesome!* All the way to the antipodes to see a flying boater. (But will they believe you back home?)

I frowned. Why must Fedora draw so much attention to herself? When will she learn that invisibility is just not *normal*? (But who defines normal, you might ask. All I can say is, people have a lot of trouble with difference and, in the prejudice stakes, I reckon invisibility would probably rate right up there — way ahead of pit bull terriers, cloggers and coneheads.)

Another wave of commuters crashed past clutching their wallets, dreaming of baked dinners, hot baths and warm beds — but the tribal circle of life's adventurers held firm. Flinders Street Station has always been a shelter for the young and homeless — just as it has always been a fearful, alien place for the rich and security conscious.

'Tiffany 'as fire!' Fedora announced enigmatically as we fell into step. 'I 'eard 'er tell someone called Stones, or per'aps it was 'Rocks'? You 'ave so many strange names.' She smiled at me. 'I 'ope the fire is close. Your Teresa will be waiting.'

Tell me something I don't know.

A voluptuous girl in a black caftan swam upstream as we crossed against the traffic to St Paul's Cathedral, bells tinkling a rhythm from her ankles. I admired the tiny black backpack which abseiled from her shoulders, sporting a large purple sticker: 'Cheers for Queers'.

Tiffany pushed past and ran over the concrete on bare feet. I clenched my teeth and followed — tension setting in. There had to be a method to this particular madness.

An old man was poking a fire in a barrel located in the lane behind the church. It was partially hidden behind a row of benches and I was sure it was illegal, but whatever... People had to keep warm somehow and we had important work to do — hats to burn. I dropped my bike beside a heap of crumpled blankets and ripped the pannier open, aware of a chill creeping into my bones. How had it become so cold, so quickly?

Fedora had already thrown in the boater.

'Hey! What're you doing? You can't burn that!' One of

the kids bellowed — blaming the old man. 'That's a bloody good hat.' He lunged at it, burnt his finger and jumped back. 'Fuckin' waste!'

Tough. I twisted the pannier free of the bike, pulled the tie open and lifted the bag above the fire. As I shook out the four hats and watched them crumple into the orange glow, I felt a terrible remorse twist through my body. They were so beautiful; so well crafted. Grief burned my belly. Someone... had... spent... hours... days... *designing, making, sewing, glueing...* Someone... had... loved... those... hats.

I watched as the delicate green Florentine straw hat with the round crown and wide brim, covered with ostrich plumes, silk flowers and *faille moiré* ribbons in shades of rose, green and golden yellow, shimmered and glowed until it was a perfect rainbow of flame.

I stared in shock as the velour derby with the grey silk scarf, grey netting and grey burnished buckle settled itself between a burning drink carton and the black silk top hat with the dusky satin ribbon, and finally fizzled into an ugly blue-black blob of glowing garbage.

I moaned audibly as the turquoise hat, with the deep green ribbon edge and scarlet plume jumped over the top of the fire, smoking and crackling — fighting for its life.

I was in terrible pain — but it seemed to be someone else's pain. I looked up and Fedora was staring at me as if she had seen a ghost. (Ha! That's a good one.) A black-and-white rat emerged from the girl-in-black's sleeve. I was observing its soft, shiny-smooth coat from a great distance when I heard a terrified scream. It seemed to be coming from my mouth, but it couldn't be, because my lips were closed, and...

I'm not afraid of rats.

'Jeez, Lady,' the old man was saying. 'Calm down. It's only Rhiannan's pet. He won't hurt you.'

'Julie!' Fedora's voice was warm with passion and surprise. 'My love!'

Abruptly, the terrible grief released its grip and I quivered with confusion. Had Fedora just called me 'her love'? Had she fallen for me at last? But what was this...? She was stepping right past me; she was wrapping her arm around someone else; she was stroking another woman's face with her long fine fingers...

'Julie Bernard,' Fedora said in her silvery voice. 'Please allow me to present to you, your great grandmother — also known as Julie Bernard.'

… RATHER RAPIDLY

I was blinking wildly — panting like a woman in the latter stages of labour. It was all too much: a black and white rat running up and down a young woman's arm; a circle of homeless people around a barrel of fire; the resounding echo of a terrible grief. (More emotion, surely, than would seem reasonable for the demise of five beautiful hats.) A sense of desperate urgency — I had about fifteen minutes to cycle to Teresa's to prove my undying love and commitment. (It was impossible.) Fedora. (Only visible to me, of course.) And now — this newcomer.

The woman was surrounded by a strange, flashing violet aura — an intermittent halo of light — rather like that oh-so-expensive laser spire stabbing the sky from the Arts Centre. From what I could see — and it wasn't easy, because my vision was obscured by the fawning attentions of Fedora — the woman was thirty-something, wearing the sort of tailored pinstriped fine woollen suit that any lesbian would be proud to wear to a job interview. (If only she had the money.) This one had a straight skirt (you could replace that with trousers), jacket and waistcoat.

But enough about clothes — there were more important things to consider.

The woman had my *face*.

'Did you see that?' The boy with the burned fingers was saying. 'She just chucked in…'

'…a whole bunch of old hats,' the girl with the rat concluded.

'Takes all kinds,' the old man in the beanie muttered agreeably. He flicked his thumb in my direction. 'Reckon that one's away with the birdies.'

And I was. Talking to not one, but *two* ghosts.

'This has got to be the wildest stunt you've pulled yet, Fedora. Are you trying to tell me this is my great grand-mother? Well, are you? Because my great grandmother would have to be about ninety-five not out. Look at this woman — what did you say her name was — Julie? She's much too young. I mean, just because she's got my face, doesn't mean anything. Does it? Just because she's flashing strobe purple, doesn't mean she's a ghost, does it? Are you telling me she's a time-traveller, Fedora? Like you, Fedora? Is this what you're telling me? Is it?'

I was verging on hysteria, but I had chosen the right place to prattle insanely. Here in this glimmering laneway, in the sheltering arc of the burning barrel, I was just another loony let loose on the streets.

'I don't want to meet any more ghosts, Fedora. Do you hear me? Anyway, it's all over now, isn't it? We've destroyed the hats. There'll be no more murders. Case closed. The case is closed now, isn't it, Fedora?' I had come to the end of my proverbial tether. I felt I could take no more. 'I haven't got time for this, Fedora. I promised Teresa, Fedora. I've got to get home. *Now!!*'

All this time, the phosphorescent woman was sobbing into Fedora's shoulder. 'Oh, my beautiful hats, Fedora. My beautiful hats. And the rat! Did you see it? You know how much I hate rats.'

Fedora squeezed her tight. 'It's a pet, my darling. Only a tiny pet. It 'as gone now. All gone.'

'A pet,' the woman sniffed. 'Who would keep a rat as a pet?'

Fedora kissed her forehead, her cheek, her ear, her neck... (Typical butch — sees a few tears and thinks it's her big chance.) 'It is the future,' she whispered by way of explanation.

'I mean it, Fedora. I've got to go. *Now!!!*' I insisted, picking up my bicycle.

Fedora was systematically kissing her way along the woman's jawbone, heading for her lips, but just as she puckered up for the big moment, the woman pushed her to the side and smiled at me. 'Julie? Can it be? It is, isn't it? I can't believe it. Why — it must be. You look just like me.'

'You look just like me,' I repeated stupidly. For some reason my head felt too big for my helmet.

The woman's eyes moved down my body and she curled her top lip in disgust. 'Are you so very poor?'

'I'm doing all right,' I muttered defensively.

Her eyes threw a question to Fedora. 'Her clothes...'

'I've had a hard day. All right?'

The woman gazed at me sympathetically for a moment. 'Yes, of course. You have been working with my love — Fedora — to stop these terrible things happening?'

'I've been chasing hats — if that's what you mean. And I've been attacked and stabbed and a woman has been murdered. Fedora seemed to think it had something to do with those — err... *your* hats. But now they're gone. All five of them. So, if no one minds... I'm out of here.'

The crowd around the barrel seemed to be growing and all eyes were turned on me. Apparently, I was the entertainment for the night. The girl with the rat waved a plastic water bottle at me. 'Would you like a drink?'

I shook my head. She was very kind, but I was too busy for refreshments.

At this stage, my belief system was stuck somewhere between reality and pure fantasy. I was intrigued — staring at the woman Fedora said was my greatgran, waiting for more information. I was excited. I could feel answers — however bizarre — almost within my reach. But I was running out of time. The wind of doom was rushing through my belly. If I didn't start peddling, my relationship would be down the proverbial gurgler.

'Five hats?' Greatgran said. 'But surely, you mean *six*.' She started counting on her fingers as Fedora and I locked eyes. 'There was a boater, a straw, a derby, that lovely turquoise...'

'Yes,' Fedora cut in breathlessly. 'It was found under the body.'

'And the top hat.'

'Yes, I agreed,' clipping my strap into place.

'And the beret,' Greatgran concluded.

'*Beret!*' I squeaked. *Teresa*. 'What beret? The only beret we found was far too recent... It was a Borsalino.'

Greatgran turned to Fedora, her eyes wide. 'You did get the beret, didn't you?'

Fedora frowned. '*Oui*. Yes, I think we did get it, my darling. But it was given to Teresa — Julie's ...err... girlfriend.'

A sensation of pure terror impelled me onto my bike, but Fedora walked rather rapidly towards me and grabbed the seat. I could hear the crowd gasp as the wheels screamed and steamed and I peddled on the spot.

'We must go to save your Teresa, Julie — but not that way. There is no time for travelling through this city like snails. We must make a transfer together. *Vitement.*'

... WITH GAY ABANDON

Transfer?

Whoo-oo! No time for questions. The wave of energy tore through the handlebars like an electric shock, punching my jaw sideways. I heard a hollow clacking sound (my teeth slamming together) and then my joints did a very fine impression of rigor mortis, locking into place one after the other. In a matter of seconds, I was frozen onto my bike, the small bones of my hands glowing golden white through the illuminated scarlet of my transparent skin.

Transfer?

No time for panic. I am in a wind tunnel, my eyelids turned inside out — pasted against my eyebrows, my eyeballs doing some crazy dance on the surface of my brain. Then I am released — my body slack and soft — like putty. A moment later I am pedalling furiously and uselessly in the spinning tube of a cyclone. I note a wooden farmhouse floating in the centre of the storm. A young girl waves from the window. Far below I observe a tiny group of street dwellers huddling around a glowing furnace. Their heads are tipped skyward; their mouths hanging open.

Help?

The thought almost formed, but was immediately torn

to shreds as the twister evaporated and my body scattered into a million different directions. In retrospect, I guess it was something like bliss. A world of silence — dominated by tiny fragments of ears and hair and breasts and Blundstones floating through nothing — like so many jaffas let loose in a spaceship.

Suddenly there was a loud bang, a display of fireworks, a flash of my girlfriend's beautiful mouth screaming, and a thumping, crashing, wrenching sound followed by a tinkling of glass.

Teresa?

I opened my eyes and found myself looking rather too closely at a familiar pattern of carpet. I had fallen off my bike. My nose seemed to be broken, and I was feeling a considerable amount of pain in my right leg.

'Jesus Fucking Christ!' *That was Teresa's voice.* 'Look what you've done to our dinner!'

Oh, oh… I'd fallen off my bike in Teresa's living room.

I staggered to my feet sheepishly, touching my nose and staring at the blood on my fingers. I lifted my bike from the coffee table and concentrated on dragging a king prawn from between its spokes. *So that was a Transfer. Far out.* I looked at the Madonna clock on the mantlepiece. Twenty-two minutes past eight. I was early!!! *Cool.* It had taken less than a minute to move three suburbs. This transfer business isn't such a bad idea. Especially for a 'late person' like me. Think about it. Just seconds before you're due at an appointment, you call up the transfer fairy…

What a mess! Fedora and Greatgran were standing anxiously in the doorway, but they would have to wait. I was in enough trouble. Seafood and salad were spilled all over the floor. Glass crunched under my tyres as I steered the bike to the wall and leaned it against a bookshelf.

'I'm sorry, Terry. But we were running out of time, and ...'

'You're sorry! You're sorry! I make you a banquet. I look after your dog. I give you one more big fat chance. And what do you do? Drop through the fucking chimney! You are so fucking deluded, Julie Bernard. Look at all this! The dinner's wrecked. Who do you think you are now? Santa Dyke?'

I was hurt, I must confess. I'd been through heaven and earth (literally) to save Teresa from serious danger. But my actions were totally unappreciated. All my internal tapes started playing at once. I am unappreciated and unrespected. It doesn't matter what I do — she'll never understand me. I can never do enough. Never live up to her expectations. This relationship is fucked. Why bother? Anger boiled on the surface of my tongue. I looked around for Jodifosta. I felt miserable and unwanted. I'll show her... I could already see myself storming out into the cold cold snow with my dog, slamming the front door behind me...

But Teresa's face was softening. She was standing up. Walking toward me. 'Are you okay? You're bleeding...'

'*The beret! The beret!*' Fedora and Greatgran screamed.

The dark shadow of a large hand was hovering near Teresa, and as I looked up it began to slither over the wall towards her face. Now the huge fingers were curling into a fist — a fist the size of a soccer ball.

'*Terry!*' I lunged desperately. I had to remove that beret from her head. My darling Teresa! I knew only too well what terrible fate could befall anyone found wearing one of my greatgran's old hats.

... ME TO THE ALTAR

Unfortunately, the fist and I arrived at pretty much the same time, jointly knocking poor Terry backwards, so that her jaw spun, she banged against the arm of the couch, her knees buckled and we tumbled down to bounce on the rectangle of polished wood together.

'Jesus F Christ. Get off me, Julie! Have you lost your mind?'

Teresa's screams were muffled by that familiar suffocating blackness. She sounded like a mouse on helium. I fought to remain alert, but that terrifying *feeling* was already tightening itself around my neck like a deathly woollen scarf. Terry was struggling beneath me, confusion and panic driving every flex of muscle. Poor Terry — being overpowered — or 'taken' (as they are so fond of calling it in Mills & Boon circles), has never been one of her favourite games.

But I didn't have time to worry about *that*. We were both running out of air... running out of time. The bastard was strangling us. We were bound together like two dying caterpillars in a hot cocoon — entwined like twin mummies embalmed for burial. I was drowning in the dark and I could feel Terry's body going limp beneath me, her arm twitching convulsively.

Terry was dying.

Well, bugger that for a joke. I knew this guy. This *murderer* and I had danced before. And deep down (in the Jungian land of instincts) — I knew he was flesh and blood just like me. My foot had made physical contact in the alley. I had heard him speak. He had a pretty ordinary European accent. In fact, take away all these supernatural antics, and this creep was just an ordinary bloke — like any Tomas, Ricardo or Horatio. He may have been a man of few words, but each word was carved indelibly into my memory bank: *Give...me...back...my... love*. Well, he could bloody well give *me* back *my* love. No one, but *no one*, was wiping out my Teresa.

Not while I was alive, anyway!

I held what little breath I had left and willed myself to move. At school, I had always excelled at swimming underwater. All I had to do was forget my panic and concentrate on breaking away from this terrifying, suffocating grip. I could do it — and I would, by sheer determination — and perhaps a little help from my friends. In the dim horizon of my consciousness, I could hear Fedora's voice cheering me on: *Julie! Julie!* And for a mad moment I thought I made out Greatgran's voice, calling: *Use the force, Julie. Use the Force.*

I had to be hallucinating.

Whatever. Something worked, because instinctively I began to focus on compressing all of my feelings into one magnificent pinprick of power. Somehow I knew what to do. I had to break through that time screen. If I could just create one tiny hole...

I concentrated — channelling all of my protective impulses (known oh-so intimately to every butch who has ever looked out for her femme), calling up all the essential female mother/child strengths (Demeter, help me out here!), falling back on my woman-as-detective resilience, patience and determination (all my old mates — V I Warshawski, Kinsey Millhone, Miss Marple, Kay Scarpetta... flashed before my eyes.) — and finally — in a split nanosecond and a moment of true inspiration — reaching back into history, appealing to a random kaleidoscope of amazon role-models.

I am Artemis. Athena. Antiope. Aphrodite. Hippolyta. Ishtar. Isis. Medusa. I am Sigourney Weaver plunging into the underworld in Alien II. I am Xena Warrior Woman. Hear me roar. Thousands of voices howled and vibrated and shrieked and wailed, filling and expanding the tiny living room in inner city Melbourne.

I was pushing against an invisible powerful force and I was working with very little oxygen, but I was stubborn. After all, Teresa's life depended on my efforts. I dug in my metaphorical heels and held my ground — despite the fact that I felt as if I had begun a gym program set for a young Arnold Schwarzenegger. I would never give up. Nothing but blackness to work with, but somehow my mind's probe kept moving — insisting — gradually clearing a path through time and space. My psychic fingers became tentacles, stretching blindly — reaching, searching for something, *anything* ...

Suddenly, I made contact. Human hair! I was almost ecstatic with joy. A superhuman effort and I was tugging as hard as I could. But it was a thin, sticky string — cutting into my hand. Soon I would burst for lack of air. I flicked my arm to the right, then back again, looping the hair around my wrist. I strained, clenched my teeth... and there was a sudden sense of release. Light flooded the room. The blindfold was lifted. I felt a tremor of life from Terry's body beneath me and renewed my efforts.

First a ripple appeared mid-air — between my bicycle and the bookshelf. I felt a shot of triumph. Blood was pouring from my wrist where the string — which was as strong as nylon fishing line, was tearing my skin... but I knew I had him.

He was hooked.

Honestly — the process was almost as disgusting as

pulling a clump of greasy hair through a giant plughole. But I persisted. The air shifted and groaned and spat and bubbled and burped, until... erupting from the vortex burst a man of about thirty — a well-dressed, balding, freckle-faced man with a neatly trimmed red beard.

The final tug drew me upright. Then the line broke. We were finally face to face. I gasped. Air. Wonderful, fresh air.

Teresa was gulping and choking behind me. I heard her rise to her feet. I felt her lean her warm *live* body against me and I wrapped one arm around her waist, but I kept my eyes firmly fixed on Freckles. *One move and you're dead, mate.*

'Where did he come from?' Teresa groaned. 'Julie — who...' Teresa's voice was a whisper of disbelief. 'Who are those two women standing in the kitchen?'

Greatgran was smiling warmly at Teresa. 'So this is your little wife, Julie. She's very beautiful. Well, aren't you going to introduce me?'

... OUT OF MY LIFE

'*Pierre Montenegro!*' Fedora screamed. 'So it was you. You... you crazy mad man. What 'ave you done? You must let go...'

'I want only what is mine,' the man with the red hair hissed, his mouth spraying saliva. I shuddered, remembering his attack in the city laneway. *Breath like an old fart.* His lips were thick and red. He swayed a little. He seemed to be having a problem maintaining his balance. 'My 'eart 'as been broken,' he moaned.

Tell someone who cares.

'That's not all that'll be broken if you try anything,' I threatened in a steel-jaw John Wayne voice. Was it my imagination, or were his freckles flashing a dull green? 'Who is this guy, Fedora?'

'This is my house!' Teresa shrieked in frustration. 'What do you all mean — barging in here...?' She was blinking furiously, holding back the tears. Then she remembered her manners. She turned to Fedora and Greatgran. 'I am Teresa — Julie's... err...' She seemed to be making a decision. 'Julie's partner.'

A shot of joy nagged at my lips. *Yay. I'm back.*

Greatgran was across the room in less time than it takes to say 'time travel'. 'I am so pleased to meet you, Teresa. So happy for you both. I am Julie's great grandmother — visiting from the past. And this is Fedora Walker... my... err... my wife.' She kissed the air beside Teresa's ears.

Fedora's elegantly gloved hand took hold of Teresa's. As usual, she was all style and grace, despite the urgency of the situation. ''allo Teresa. I am Julie's client. We 'ave met before actually, but... err... I think you do not see me.'

Teresa leaned against the mantlepiece. 'You mean... You're the *ghost?*' She looked at me in astonishment. 'It was all *true.*'

I nodded.

Fedora nodded.

Greatgran nodded.

Soon, we were all nodding. Even Teresa was thoughtfully lifting her head up and down. It was one of those fabulous I-was-right-and-you-were-wrong moments.

A moment I will hang on to forever.

We were so busy nodding, we forgot about Freckles. Suddenly, he lunged at the beret, lying forgotten near the couch. But he slipped and fell, diving into a pile of spilled potato salad and skidding across the carpet. Greatgran's tiny boot stamped angrily on his hand. 'You have done quite enough, Pierre. Go away now, please. I want to talk to my great granddaughter.'

'Pierre?' I repeated. I was still groping in the dark.

'It is mine. Give... it... to... me.'

'Oh, don't be ridiculous,' Greatgran said matter-of-factly. 'You didn't design that beret. You were long dead when my daughter-in-law bought that one. It just got mixed up in the collection — over the years. You've been raging away on the threshold for so long, you've lost your reason — *and* your memory.'

'That beret belongs to Teresa,' I said, snatching it up and shaking off a dust ball. 'It was a gift from me. It's a Borsalino...' (I'm such a show-off).

Freckles gazed at me in appeal as he pulled himself to his knees. 'Are you a milliner *aussi, Mademoiselle?*' Why did his voice have that distant, hollow sound? And why were his freckles now shining a sickly iridescent yellow? (I've heard of people with an inner glow, but this bloke?)

'Did you really do all this... just for a couple of your *hats?*'

'Miss Bernhardt's hats,' Freckles corrected sadly.

I had a million questions, but Teresa intervened. 'Is this the man who murdered Lily? Shouldn't we call the police?'

'There is no need for that,' Greatgran said with satisfaction. 'Pierre will find punishment enough on the other side.'

Realisation dawned as Freckles looked down at his hands and saw the rapidly multiplying tubes of penetrating light. He looked like a colander held against the sun, each freckle opening slowly to release little searchlights from another world. '*No-o-o-o!*' he screamed.

'Pierre can do no more 'arm,' Fedora reassured us with a chummy smile.

'No,' Greatgran agreed. 'But he may have been hiding in the threshold forever — if Julie hadn't pulled him from his closet.'

Fedora shook her head in disapproval. ''iding in the closet, Pierre. You were always such a coward.'

'I'm so proud of you, my darling,' Greatgran said. I did a double take. Could it be true? Yes. Greatgran was smiling in my direction. My great grandmother was proud — of me. I felt quite intoxicated. (I think I mentioned it before — not that I'm permanently traumatised or obsessed or anything — but the word 'proud' has never been a part of my mother's vocabulary.)

'Julie is an 'ero!' Fedora announced.

'And now — Pierre Montenegro must go to meet his fate,' Greatgran added with satisfaction.

I sensed what was going to happen next. Not that I'm psychic — I'm just a bit of a media freak. I've watched the X-files. I saw *Dracula* just the other night at Johnny's place. I loved *The Hunger*. (Catherine Deneuve. Mm. Another French woman. Am I obsessed?) I know that dead vampires can dissolve to dust and live vampires can turn themselves into hundreds of rats. But I knew Terry was scared of horror films. So I wrapped her in my arms and waited for the action.

Freckles was writhing in pain. His legs extended into the splits, then wound like snakes around his neck. His arms were spinning away from his shoulders. Suddenly, he did a series of cartwheels on the spot, whirling and blurring like one of those fancy fireworks you attach to a fence. He was Rubber Man from an ancient side-show; he was a circus acrobat in a hurry. 'Help me!' he implored, holding out a ragged hand. 'Help me!'

Teresa looked from him to me, her eyes rolling in

disgust and fear. I squeezed her tight, one arm lifting her breasts. For some reason, I felt totally unafraid. Must have been all that praise from Greatgran and Fedora. *Julie is an 'ero!* I could feel Teresa's heart thumping. Her fingernails were biting into my flesh. Her skin was damp with fear. I pressed my groin against her hip and felt a shot of excitement.

S'pose a fuck's out of the question?

Ohmigod! Did I say that out loud?

'Cover your eyes,' Greatgran yelled — just before the explosion.

... WITH ME

My ears ached with the crash of a million gigantic bells. Radiant light bleached all colour from the room. Through my narrowed eyes, I saw the man with the red hair begin to shrivel, his freckles popping — bones snapping and crackling as the Great Laundry Woman in the sky folded him into smaller and smaller squares. Eventually, he became a tiny squealing blowfly zipping blindly around the room. Once he banged against the window; twice he bounced against the Lady Lamp. And there he was, hovering mid-air — vibrating just above Fedora's head.

Teresa and I clung together in a frozen embrace — our eyes fixed on the human helicopter.

'Get over it, Pierre,' Greatgran said. (I love that woman.)

Fedora sighed. She lifted one gloved hand and pushed the air gently. Immediately, the spot rippled and spun and sparkled until it became a red spiralling abyss. One tiny gulp and Pierre disappeared. Fedora waved her hand in farewell, smoothing the air as if it were a pillow. Then everything fell back into place, the bookshelf jumping into vibrant technicolor.

'Wow!' I said. 'That was great.'

Greatgran rubbed her eyes. 'Reversals are always so *dramatic!*'

Slowly, Teresa unwrapped her limbs from around my body. 'Who was that man?' she whispered.

'We must talk, *vitement*,' Fedora ordered. 'Before it is time for us to go... *aussi*.'

I felt a surge of woman-as-detective excitement, mixed with a terrible sadness. Fedora was leaving. I leaned my elbow on the mantelpiece and crossed one foot in front of the other. (I've read Agatha Christie. I know the resolution is on its way when the facts begin to emerge in front of the fireplace.)

'What do you mean: 'Time to go'?'

'It is all done,' Fedora said. 'There will be no more murders.'

I had a terrifying image of Fedora and Greatgran as tiny folded sheets. 'Are you going — where he...?'

'No, Julie,' Greatgran smiled. 'We have crossed only bridges — not borders. Not like Pierre. We will be return- ing to our own time.'

'When is your... err... time?' Teresa asked. (She was doing a good job of keeping it together, considering everything.)

'The twenty-fourth of April, nineteen hundred and three,' Greatgran replied. 'Fedora and I are thinking of moving to Paris next month. It will be our eleventh anniversary.' Greatgran's hand slid into Fedora's. 'Quite the old married couple.'

'But Greatgran — do you mind if I call you that? You had five kids, didn't you? At least that's what I've been told... According to the family records — my Poppa, Dad's dad... He was your little baby... Percival. Isn't that right?'

'Darling little Percy.'

The idea of my grizzly old grandfather as someone's 'darling little Percy' had never occurred to me. 'What did he think about Fedora? How come my Dad never said any...'

'Oh, for heaven's sakes,' Greatgran interrupted impatiently. 'You must ask the right questions. Everyone has an aunt or a grandmother like me — *somewhere* in the records.'

'But five kids...?' My head was spinning.

Greatgran's mouth fell open. 'Don't they allow inverts to have children in your time?'

'Why was that man so crazy about a few hats?' Teresa asked suddenly.

Greatgran returned to the matter at hand. 'Those hats were a gift... a precious gift — from Sarah Bernhardt. She gave them to me when she was on tour in Australia. But then, of course, there was one person who was not happy when she arrived home in Paris — without her hats.'

Fedora nodded in agreement. 'Not 'appy at all.'

I nodded, 'appy that the pieces were falling neatly into place. 'Pierre Montenegro.'

''e was mad with the jealousy.'

Greatgran lowered her voice conspiratorially. 'You see — Monsieur Montenegro made those hats especially for Sarah. He was the best milliner in Paris and he was crazy with love for Sarah Bernhardt.'

'Over the moon in love,' Fedora clarified.

'Of course she was never the slightest bit interested.'

''e did not exist for 'er... But 'e was crazy with jealousy.'

'Like a madman. He demanded to know…'

'…where had Sarah left her 'ats,' Fedora concluded. 'But of c ourse Sarah 'ad left 'er 'ats with my love in Australia. *That* is where.'

I hate talking to the two-headed couple-monster, don't you? My neck was already beginning to ache — as my head swivelled from Greatgran to Fedora and back to Greatgran.

'So Sarah refused to tell him?'

'She did not want 'im!' Fedora continued emphatically. 'She did not want 'is 'ats. Nothing to make 'er think of this man. Meantime Pierre was becoming tiresome — following her everywhere — living in a fantasy of 'ope.'

'A stalker,' Teresa said, nodding.

'But Sarah 'oped too. She 'oped — if she gave the 'ats away — she would be able to forget 'im and 'is stupid dreamings.'

I was intrigued. 'Why do you speak of yourself in the third person? You speak as though Sarah were someone else.'

'Yes?' Fedora said, puzzled.

'Aren't *you* Sarah Berhardt?'

Greatgran and Fedora exchanged a look and then burst into laughter. They giggled and gurgled and clutched one another, staggering hysterically.

'Get over it,' I muttered crossly.

Terry took my hand; I think she was feeling protective.

'I'm sorry,' Greatgran sputtered. 'Of course, you would think Fedora was Sarah.' She kissed Fedora affectionately on the cheek. 'Fedora was never good at explanations, were you darling? Of course, Fedora is not Sarah and Sarah is not Fedora. Fedora is a character in a play, which

Emile Sardou wrote for Sarah Bernhardt. You must have heard of him — of his play — *Fedora?*'

'Yes,' Terry said. 'It's on in town at the moment.'

That mist was descending over my world again — just when things were becoming clear.

'I was in love with Sarah,' Greatgran continued, 'but only the Sarah I saw on the stage. Night after night, I made my way to watch the divine Sarah Bernhardt, and one evening — backstage — she gave me the basket of hats. I was so happy — but even then, I knew that to her I was just another Australian fan. I knew she would never really notice me...'

Fedora's hand ran across Greatgran's back, her fingers resting gracefully on one shoulder. Greatgran's face was alight with love. 'Then... on one very special night, Sarah looked out into the audience and she saw me. I willed it — I'm sure. I was so taken with her — I had never seen anyone like her before. And at the end of the play, when Sarah walked off stage... There was Fedora. Still there — staring at me.'

'That's so romantic,' Teresa said, sniffing and searching my pocket for a handkerchief.

'Fedora was always ...err... a little disembodied,' Greatgran said proudly. 'And that's been a big help with all this time travel. Without her abilities, Pierre would have continued killing until my hats fell apart from old age. But Fedora couldn't have done it without you, my beautiful granddaughter. You were home to her homing pigeon. Fedora knew me, and because you were my namesake... And I was Sarah's mother's namesake...'

'Three is a very powerful number,' Teresa agreed. She seemed to be looking at me with new interest.

'Why — when we found out you were working as a detective — we thought all our Christmases had come at once.'

'But now we must go, Julie,' Fedora said. 'Do I owe you...?'

I shook my head, lost for words. Who could think of finances at a time like this? Greatgran and Fedora were disintegrating in front of my eyes. I wanted to sob; my throat was bursting.

'Will... I... ever... see... you... again?'

'Of course, Julie. Just... call... your... name...,' Fedora sang from the threshold.

'Julie Bernard.

Julie Bernard

Julie...'

RELATED TITLES FROM SPINIFEX PRESS

Finola Moorhead
darkness more visible
An epic novel of sudden death, cyberconspiracy and possibly crime, set on the lesbianlands of New South Wales.
ISBN: 1-875559-60-4

Gillian Hanscombe
Figments of Murder
Babes is the hero ofthe London women's movement. And a target. A passionate and satirical novel about betrayal and lust.
ISBN: 1-875559-43-4

Melissa Chan
Too Rich
You can never bee too thin or too rich. Or can you? Francesca Miles, independent feminist detective finds out.
ISBN: 1-875559-02-7

Beryl Fletcher
The Bloodwood Clan
An intriguing tale of secrecy, politics, religious funda-mentalism and racial intolerance.
ISBN: 1-875559-80-9

*If you would like to know more about Spinifex Press,
write for a free catalogue or visit our Website.*

SPINIFEX PRESS
PO Box 212, North Melbourne
Victoria 3051 Australia
<http://www.spinifexpress.com.au>